The Kiskadee of Death

The Bob White Birder Murder Mysteries

The Boreal Owl Murder

Murder on Warbler Weekend

A Bobwhite Killing

Falcon Finale

A Murder of Crows

Swift Justice

Visit Jan online at www.jandunlap.com for more about the Birder Murders, and like her Birder Murder Mama author page on Facebook!

The Kiskadee of Death

Jan Dunlap

North Star Press of St. Cloud, Inc.
Saint Cloud, Minnesota

ISBN 978-0-87839-799-0

First Edition: September 2015

Printed in the United States of America

Published by
North Star Press of St. Cloud, Inc.
P.O. Box 451
St. Cloud, Minnesota 56302

www.northstarpress.com

Chapter One

One of the best things about birding is that there are always birds somewhere to be seen.

For example, even in the dead of winter in Minnesota, you can find species of ducks or gulls that have wandered down from the Arctic to add to your life list, which is always a thrill for a birder. You might have to shovel a ton of snow off your car before you can set out to see a rarity, or put on five layers of clothing so you don't freeze to death while you're looking for the bird, but we Minnesotan birders have learned to accept the hardships of our hobby.

Some of us have also learned that our native birds are a lot smarter than we are—after all, they fly south for the winter every year, along with most of the state's retirees. While we poor working Joes, like me, are struggling through snowdrifts on a daily basis, Minnesota's migrants of the human and feathered types are catching rays in the Yucatan and ordering drinks from cabana boys.

"Make that a piña colada for me and a splash of water in the birdbath for the warblers, please."

Which was why I decided to take a tip from our Minnesota snowbirds of both persuasions and head south to warmer climes after the thermometer on my back deck stopped working when it hit the eighth day of sub-zero highs in January.

"Honey, we're heading to the Lower Rio Grande Valley in Texas," I told my wife, Luce, over the lemon mousse she'd prepared for dessert after dinner. "With windchills expected in the negative forties next week, school will be cancelled anyway. If I add a few of the vacation days I've got coming, we can be spending a week in shorts and tee-shirts, watching Great Kiskadees and Green Jays from Harlingen to McAllen to Mission. What do you say?"

Luce took a bite of her mousse and considered my offer.

"It's my early Valentine's gift to you," I prompted. "Don't look a gift horse in the mouth, Luce, especially one that wants to carry you away from the bitter cold."

She gave me a glare and then pointed with her spoon at the mousse in front of her. "Only if I can bring back a crate of lemons fresh from the tree," she said. "Because if I have to use one more left-over-from-last-season, tasteless lemon in my kitchen this month, I'll throw my juicer out the window and set fire to my favorite vinaigrette recipes file."

Since my wife's a professional chef—and I get to eat like a king because of it—the idea of her tossing in the dishtowel is never a comforting thought as far as I'm concerned. Our mutual passion for birds may have been the first sticks in building the cozy nest of our relationship, but Luce's amazing cooking skills were some of the saliva that held it together.

Oh, wait. Maybe that imagery doesn't work for you. It's a bird thing, you know—constructing nests with saliva. But I digress . . .

"We can arrange that," I promised her, already planning our driving route south in my head. "I'll personally pack all the fresh citrus you want into the car for our ride back home."

I lifted my own spoon of mousse in salute.

"Lower Rio Grande Valley, here we come! Great Kiskadees, Green Jays, and fresh lemons await!"

Good thing I didn't know then what else we were going to find in Texas on our spur-of-the-moment birding get-away, and I'm not referring to the shortage of parking spaces around the annual Citrus Festival Parade we ended up attending in the American border town of Mission, either.

Limited parking was nothing compared to having handcuffs snapped on my wrists for assault with a deadly weapon.

Yee-haw.

* * *

"We haven't missed our turn, have we?"

Luce peered at the asphalt road ahead of us that seemed to lead straight to the Mexican border. It was Wednesday, our third morning of birding along the Lower Rio Grande Valley, and we were looking for the entrance to the World Birding Center's Estero Llano Grande State Park to try to add a Green Kingfisher to our bird list for the week.

"I don't think so," I replied, taking a quick glance at my odometer. "I think we've got another third of a mile before the turn. Based on how little signage we've seen this week for the parks and birding centers, though, I'm beginning to wonder if Texas birders would just as soon keep the birds to themselves."

I adjusted my front window visor to reduce the morning sun's glare. The flat land of the valley stretched out on all sides of us, with occasional palm trees dotting the landscape, along with mesquite, yuccas, and willows.

"I doubt that," Luce said, "given that birding and birding-related tourism seems to be the biggest economic engine in this area. I don't think I've ever visited a place where more people are talking about birds than they are here. It really is a birder's paradise. There," she added, pointing to an approaching fork in the road. "That's the left turn to the park. There's even a sign for you."

I signaled my turn and drove into the half-full parking lot at the entrance to Estero Llano Grande State Park. Luce and I got out of the car, enjoying the warmth of the air and the sunshine on our bare arms.

"I think I could get used to seventy-degree weather in January," I said, "not to mention dry roads. It makes birding a lot more fun when you don't have to battle windchills and blizzards to add birds to your life list."

I held out my hand for the bottle of sunscreen Luce was squirting along her long, albeit Minnesota fish-white, lovely legs.

She passed the bottle to me over the front hood of the car, and I dutifully applied a thick coating across my arms, nose, cheeks, and the back of my neck. I tossed the bottle back in the car and pulled out my backpack, which was already loaded with binoculars, bird guides, a camera, and water bottles. I slipped my arms through the straps and shrugged it snug against my back. Luce came around the front of the car and wiped a smudge of sunscreen off my cheek, then dropped a kiss on my lips.

"I'm so glad you talked me into this trip," she said. "Not that you had to try very hard," she admitted. "I was just so ready for a change of scene. I was beginning to think I was going crazy."

I returned her kiss with one of my own. "Yeah, I sort of figured that out when you threatened to burn your recipe books and only eat fast food for the next month. You hate fast food."

Luce shook her head in dismay.

"I don't know what came over me," she confessed. "I just haven't felt like myself for a while. Winter can be wicked, but vacation is a wonderful thing," she concluded, adjusting her new ball cap on her head.

A Great Kiskadee and a Green Jay—regular species in the Lower Rio Grande Valley—were embroidered on the hat. "I feel like a whole new woman," Luce announced.

"What was wrong with the old woman?" I asked. "I thought she was pretty nice, except for the fast food threat. That was scary."

Luce laughed and wrapped her hand around my bicep. "I bet it was. But I don't want to think about cooking today, Bobby. Let's go find that Green Kingfisher for you."

We crossed the parking lot to a brick-paved path that wound through a garden of palms and thick vegetation to a large viewing deck that adjoined the Visitor's Center. Beyond the deck lay a broad pond, currently hosting a multitude of Ruddy Ducks, Soras, Gadwalls, Common Gallinules and American Coots. I lifted my binoculars to my eyes and quickly picked out a pair of Mottled Ducks, along with both a Blue-winged Teal and a Green-winged Teal floating nearby.

"We had thirty species this morning by 9:45," said a petite woman standing near the rail of the deck. Her voice carried the lilt of the Hispanic accent that we'd found so common in this local stretch of southern Texas towns from Brownsville to Rio Grande City.

I lowered my binos and looked her way. Like many a birder, she wore khaki shorts, a loose cotton shirt, and a floppy hat that shielded her face from the bright morning sun. Binoculars hung from a strap around her neck, and I guessed she was in her late sixties judging from the wisps of black and silver hair that framed her face below her hat brim.

"I'd call that a good morning for birding," I told her.

"*No esta* bad," the woman replied.

When she caught my momentary look of confusion, she smiled.

"It's not bad," she said, translating her bit of Spanish into English for us.

I returned her smile. "Spanglish, right?"

She nodded. "Yes. You know it?"

"We're learning," Luce assured her.

Like so many people we'd met in the Valley since our arrival, the woman's comment had been a mix of Spanish and English words. Known as 'Spanglish,' it was one more unique characteristic of the area that blended together Hispanic and American culture. I was getting more comfortable hearing it in casual conversation, and I was even picking up a few Spanish words myself, but it still took me a second to catch on and process the two-language combination.

"We've had a total of 326 species seen here in the course of the year," our new acquaintance said.

She moved towards me and extended her hand to shake mine. "I'm Rosalie. Welcome. I'm one of the volunteer naturalists here. I help visitors with bird identification."

"Bob White," I told her, and nodded toward Luce, who was studying the pond through her own binos. "My wife, Luce."

"Luce?" Rosalie tilted her head to the side, reminding me of a quick little wren eyeing an insect. "Is that short for Lucy?"

"No," my wife explained, turning away from scanning the pond. "It's short for Lucia. My parents named me for the Swedish Saint Lucia. A lot of people mispronounce Lucia, so I go by Luce."

Rosalie clasped her hands in front of her chest, her voice filled with delight. "*Es un nombre precioso.* A lovely name! And it carries your heritage. You are Swedish, no?"

Luce smiled. "My grandmother is Swedish. I'm American."

Rosalie proudly patted her own chest with both hands. "I was born in Mexico, but I am an American now. My children—they are all Americans."

I pointed to an oversized chalkboard lying across the top of a large circular table on the deck beside Rosalie. "Is that a bird list?"

Rosalie nodded briskly. "That's our list from this morning. I had a group of twenty birders out here an hour ago. Is this your first visit to Estero Llano?"

"It is," Luce answered her. "We birded the Santa Ana National Wildlife Refuge yesterday, and the day before that, we spent the morning at the Bentsen-Rio Grande State Park."

"Ah," Rosalie commented with a friendly smile, "you are making the rounds of our parks. There is so much to see here, no?"

"Too much," I told her. "We've already decided we're going to have to make the trip again. Once is definitely not enough to thoroughly explore all the birding sites around here."

That was an understatement.

In just two days, Luce and I had already added nineteen birds to our life lists, and those were all birds that were common residents of the area, known collectively as "Valley specialties." There were still another twelve or so "specialties" we had yet to see, but I was hopeful we'd get them all before heading north in another three days.

Seeing Valley specialties wasn't the extent of the birding we'd found here, either. The Lower Rio Grande Valley is where two major migratory corridors—the Central and Mississippi—converge, making it the best place in the United States to see more than 500 species of birds.

Not only that, but the Valley is also the meeting point of four different climate zones—temperate, desert, coastal and sub-tropical—along with the birds who thrive in them. Throw in the South and Central American birds whose northernmost range ends at the Rio Grande, and a Minnesotan like me can potentially see birds I've only dreamed about.

And believe me, I've dreamed about a lot of birds.

That's why I was already planning our next trip to the Valley.

"They had a Virginia Rail this morning, Bobby." Luce pointed at one of the items on the chalkboard list.

"It's one of our winter visitors," Rosalie noted. "Not one of the most visible ones, to be sure, but we're always happy when it makes an appearance."

"I can imagine," I said. Rails are notorious for their birder-avoidance, and the marsh in front of us was a perfect habitat for them with the lush vegetation around it. "I'm hoping we catch a glimpse of one while we're in the area this week," I told Rosalie, "but so far, no luck."

"Are you making the grand tour of the nine World Birding Centers, then?" Rosalie asked.

"Trying to," Luce said. "But we need at least a couple weeks more to even begin doing justice to all the species here. The birding is amazing."

"And this isn't even migration season," Rosalie pointed out. "You probably already know that we sit at the convergence of two major migratory corridors."

I nodded. "Yes, we know."

Seriously, I didn't think any birder to the area *couldn't* know that fact—every park we visited had displays about the Central and Mississippi flyways joining up in the Lower Rio Grande Valley. I'd always thought Minnesotans were proud of sitting on the Mississippi migration corridor with all its own spectacular visitors, but our pride paled in comparison to the Texas birders' love of their two flyways.

"You should see this place in November," Rosalie continued. "We get busloads of birders pulling in to see our migrants. That's when we have the big Rio Grande Valley Birding Festival, too, you know."

I knew that, too. The event had been on my wish list for years, but I had yet to attend the RGVBF—being a high school counselor tended to put a crimp in any travel plans I might try to hatch between August and December. From what other birders have told me, it's a five-day birding bonanza based in the city of Harlingen, Texas, with expert-led field trips to all the World Birding Centers, along with every other nature preserve and refuge along the Lower Rio Grande. Around 1,200 birders show up for the event, which means there's a whole lot of bird-talking going on.

Yup, definitely my idea of a good time.

"So what should we absolutely not miss while we're here at Estero Llano?" Luce asked Rosalie.

"Well, if you haven't seen a Common Pauraque yet, there's one that frequents the trails on the far side of Alligator Lake," Rosalie suggested. "Pauraques spend most of their time on the ground, and since they're a nightjar species, they're active at night, feeding on insects, so you'll have to look pretty closely to find one during the day. Also, it has great natural camouflage; its feathers make it almost invisible among the leaves and sticks on the ground."

"So we better not step on one, right?" I joked.

"You may laugh," Rosalie responded, "but the fact is, Common Pauraques often choose to run, rather than fly, from predators. In fact, in areas where there are a lot of feral cats or dogs, the Pauraque population doesn't last long. So, yes," she smiled. "Please don't step on the Pauraques."

"Anything else we should be looking for?" Luce asked.

Rosalie looked out over the pond and pursed her lips. "Well, there is a one-eyed Great Kiskadee that's been showing up around the Valley. We haven't added it to our new species list yet, but you never know."

She winked to assure us she was joking.

"Hey, Rosie!"

I turned to see a tall, broad-shouldered man, likewise dressed in khaki shorts and a floppy hat. He'd just stepped onto the deck from a trail on its east side, and he was heading our way. Even from a distance, I could tell he was an older fellow, judging from his leathered and lined face and the bushy white eyebrows that rose over his eyes. Binoculars hung around his neck and a backpack was slung over his right shoulder, and he carried a tall walking stick topped with what looked like part of a deer antler. He didn't seem unsteady on his feet as he crossed the deck with a sure, long stride, so I guessed the walking stick was more for show than balance.

In fact, the closer he got to us, the more I was impressed with his straight posture and the lean muscles flexing in his legs. The man clearly kept himself in shape.

"Hey, Buzz," Rosalie called back, "did you see the Pauraque this morning?"

"Not this morning," the man told Rosalie. "Ask Birdy when he gets back. He was going to check out Alligator Lake. He said he was working on a park rarity for you. I headed over to Wader's Trail to see the White-faced Ibis chicks, and got an unexpected treat myself—an Eared Grebe. I texted Birdy and a few other birders on my cell phone to hustle over here and see it, but the grebe wasn't in the mood for company. It took off."

"An Eared Grebe?" Rosalie said. Her face lit up with anticipation just before it crumpled in despair. "Gone?"

I had to chuckle to myself. Her expressions and tone of voice were as familiar to me as if I'd known her all my life. Every birder knows what it feels like to hear about a rare bird . . . that you just missed seeing. It's like finding out that the person who was in front of you in a line to buy a lotto ticket at the gas station just won the jackpot.

So close, and yet so, so far away.

"Afraid so," Buzz said. "You're not the only one who missed out, Rosie. Cynnie Scott was on her way when I texted her back that the grebe was gone. She's probably going to hold it against me personally, along with a host of other things."

He stamped his big walking stick on the park deck to dislodge a few leaves that had stuck to its bottom.

"What can I say?" he said. "All's fair in love and birding, right? You don't always get what you want, but you generally end up with what you need."

Rosalie seemed to consider her answer for a moment or two before she conceded.

"I suppose that's true," she said, though I thought I detected a decidedly uncertain note in her voice. It was gone with her next comment, however, as her voice took on a teasing tone. "I bet, right now, Cynnie would not agree with that."

Rosalie suddenly seemed to realize Luce and I were still standing nearby, and she let the subject drop in order to bring Luce and me back into the conversation.

"Buzz and Birdy are two of our favorite Winter Texans at Estero Llano," Rosalie explained to us. "They've been coming down here every winter for the last thirty years or so, and everyone knows that if it's Wednesday, you can find Buzz and Birdy scouting the trails as soon as it is light. They know this park like they were born and raised here."

"I wish I had been, but I wasn't," Buzz told us as he pulled a water bottle from his backpack and unscrewed its top. "I'm a Kansas boy originally," he said, lifting his bottle in salute. "Name's Buzz Davis. But I don't think I can qualify as a Winter Texan anymore," he added, "since I bought a home here two years ago. The city of Mission is my home now."

I waited till he finished his drink, then introduced myself and Luce.

"Nice to meet you," the new Texan said. Like every other Texan we'd met on our trip, he made sure to shake our hands in greeting and welcome us to the state. "Where are you folks from?"

"We're fugitives from the frozen north," I explained. "We live in Minnesota, just outside the Twin Cities. We decided we'd come and see how the warmer half of the United States lives."

Buzz laughed, deep lines crinkling around his startling blue eyes.

"I don't know if Texas qualifies for half of the U.S., though I'm sure you can find some native sons who would be pleased as punch to hear you say that," he said. "The natives down here think that the sun rises and sets in Texas, don't they, Rosie?"

He threw a broad wink at the volunteer naturalist, who responded with a polite smile.

"I'm guessing this is your first trip," he continued, returning his attention to me and Luce, "if Rosie here is sending you out to find the Pauraque. It's one of Estero Llano's park specialties, since around here is about the only place in North America where you can count on finding it. Otherwise, you'd have to go to Central or South America to see it. It's one of those lucky migrants that's actually . . . welcomed . . . when it crosses the border here."

His emphasis on the word "welcomed" caught my ear and sent a tickle of awareness down my spine.

Unless I misread his vocal inflection, the man wasn't just talking about birds.

He was making a reference to what Luce and I had already found to be one of the standard topics of conversation in southern Texas: illegal immigration.

And while I'd always made it a policy to try to keep politics out of my birding excursions, I'd found in the last few days it was almost impossible to do that in the Lower Rio Grande Valley. Local birders had almost as many stories to tell about immigration busts as they did about rare bird sightings. Most of the birders who had mentioned it to us were of the opinion that illegal immigration activity was simply a fact of life along the border corridor, and as long as they stayed focused on birds and not political issues, they could continue to bird in peace.

No reason to stir up a potential hornets' nest, especially when access to so many species of birds was at stake. Birders might have tunnel vision when it comes to their hobby, but they're certainly not blind to circumstances that might restrict that vision.

Buzz Davis, however, didn't seem shy at all about broaching the topic.

Out of curiosity, I glanced at Rosalie for her reaction to Buzz's comment, but she was suddenly intent on moving us along on our birding objective.

"If you want to see the Pauraque, you should probably get going over that way," she said, ignoring Buzz and pointing to where he'd accessed the deck. "The bird gets harder to pick out from the vegetation along the trails when the sun is higher overhead. You lose the definition you get with shadows."

Since Buzz didn't add anything, and Rosalie bent over her chalkboard to update her observations, I looked at Luce and tipped my head in the direction Rosalie had indicated. "Shall we?"

"Sure," Luce said, reaching for my hand. We walked off the deck and followed a sign that marked the way to Alligator Lake.

"Over there," I said, suddenly stopping and lifting my binoculars to my eyes. "On that feeding platform. That's a female Vermilion Flycatcher."

Luce followed my gaze and then sighted the bird through her own binoculars.

"Good eye," she said, "especially since the female only has that little bit of pale red color on her belly and undertail, unlike her hubby, who's brilliant."

Almost as if she had conjured the bird just by mentioning him, an adult male Vermilion Flycatcher flew past the feeding platform.

"Now, that is a red bird," I said. The male perched in some scrub on the edge of the trail momentarily before it sped off again in pursuit of more insects.

"I got the impression Rosalie didn't particularly appreciate the editorial comment about migrants Buzz made," Luce said, still watching the female flycatcher.

"Yup, I thought the conversation turned rather abruptly back to our birding agenda," I agreed. "Maybe the illegal immigrant issue along the border is a taboo topic for park volunteers," I speculated. "After all, how many of these World Birding Centers are within miles—at most—of the border? I'm guessing it can't be great publicity for encouraging tourism if you parade a local hot button in front of visitors. You don't hear about the drug busts until you get here, either," I pointed out. "Not that it matters. It takes a lot more than border conflicts and drug investigations to keep birders away from birds."

"Parade!" Luce exclaimed. "That's where I knew that name from."

I glanced at Luce, who had stopped in the middle of the trail.

"What are you talking about?"

"Buzz Davis!" she said. "He was an astronaut before we were born. I saw him in a parade in the Twin Cities in 2000. He was Grand Marshall of the St. Patrick's Day parade that year. He was like sixty years old then, but he sure didn't look it. Seriously, I had a crush on him for years after that."

I came back to where Luce was standing and put my hands on her shoulders.

"Are you saying I have competition for your affections?"

Luce smiled. "No. Never."

She leaned in to give me a kiss.

"Especially if you look that good when you're seventy-five, Bobby." She patted my cheek. "I'll have to beat off your admirers with a stick."

"I love it when you talk that rough stuff. Will you marry me?" I asked her.

Luce laughed. "I already did."

I slapped my head in mock surprise. "I knew you looked familiar."

Luce punched me in the shoulder and we continued walking on the hard dirt path towards Alligator Lake. A left bend in the trail led us across a small footbridge over a drainage ditch to connect with another park trail called Camino de Aves. Thorn scrub lined the sides of the ditch, with woodland stretching out beyond it in a flat expanse broken by several narrow, shallow lakes.

"Do you think there are really alligators in the lake?" Luce asked as we passed a mounted map of the park that identified our position with a yellow star. "I don't think of alligators as living in Texas," she added. "Florida, yes. Texas, no."

"Make that Texas, also yes," I said, pointing to another sign that came into view as we neared the edge of what was clearly Alligator Lake.

The sign read *Do not disturb the alligators.*

"Okay, then," Luce said. "I will definitely not disturb the alligators."

A few yards ahead of us were three men and one woman, all with binoculars trained on the opposite shore of the small lake. Like Buzz and Rosalie, they were seniors, but judging from their lack of similarly well-tanned legs and arms, I guessed they were, like Luce and me, simply passing through. It occurred to me that just as you can identify a male from a female Vermilion Flycatcher by their distinctive coloration, you could as easily tell a visiting snowbird from a local resident.

The skin of the visitor was almost as white as a freshly plucked chicken waiting for the oven, while the resident was already nicely browned.

At the moment, I myself was mid-way between the two at parboiled, thanks to the sunburn I'd gotten on Monday, our first full day of birding in Texas. At home, I usually remembered to put on the sunscreen the first time I get back outside in the spring since I've borne the curse of a redhead's fair skin my whole life and endured many a painful peeling because of it. Unfortunately, it hadn't occurred to me that I'd get sunburned in January.

Until I got sunburned . . . in January.

Not that I'm complaining. If a sunburn was the price I had to pay to bird in Texas in January, I was happy to write the check.

The day after I got the sunburn, I was also happy to buy the bottle of sunscreen I'd already used in the parking lot this morning.

I stepped closer to the tall, elderly fellow nearest me to see where the other birders in his group were aiming their binoculars. The man wore a blue-and-black bandana around his head, and a long gray ponytail trailed partway down his back.

"Yellow-crowned Night Herons," he said. "Over there on the bank."

Unlike the older birders, neither Luce nor I needed to use our binoculars to get a good look at the herons. Three were perched in tree branches that hung low over the dark water of the shallow lake, with another two posed right along the shoreline. Their pale yellow crown stripes and white cheeks made them easy to recognize, and as we watched, the two herons on the shore slowly moved into the shallows of the pond, foraging for food. Since the other birds were perched in trees, I looked for nests, knowing that, where several pairs of birds are found, it's likely that they're members of a small colony that reuses the site for many years. Instead of nests, I caught sight of another bird partially hidden back in the drooping tree branches.

"Hang on," I whispered to Luce, lifting my binos to focus in on the bird. "I think I got our Green Kingfisher."

A quick look was all I needed to make the positive ID, the bird's dark green plumage making the kingfisher almost invisible among the foliage at the edge of the lake.

"Yup, that's it," I confirmed.

The bird was about two-thirds the size of the more familiar Belted Kingfisher, but like its relative, the Green Kingfisher liked to perch while hunting for food in ponds and streams. Not only that, but the bird was generally found only in the southern half of Texas and southeast Arizona, making it the newest addition to my life list of birds.

It was another score for our trip. Texas was being very good to me.

"You see it?" I asked Luce, watching the bird through my binoculars.

"Got it," she answered.

"What? What else are you seeing?" asked the woman in the little group we'd joined. She was at least a foot shorter than I was and had to crane her neck back to see me from under her straw hat's wide brim.

I pointed across the water.

"A Green Kingfisher," I said. "Look left of the Yellow-crowned Night Heron that just picked something out of the water, then up about six feet to that big fork in the tree. The Green Kingfisher is another couple feet left of that, at about ten o'clock."

A moment of silence engulfed the group of birders while they all trained their binoculars on the spot.

"There it is," said another of the men. He, too, had a straw hat on, I noticed, but it sat atop white hair reaching the collar of his colorful shirt. "See it?"

The two other birders each affirmed the sighting.

"Thank you," said the woman in the straw hat. "That bird blends in too well for my old eyes to pick out. I never would have seen it on my own. Thank goodness you happened along."

"No problem," I replied, continuing carefully to scan the opposite shore through my binoculars. I wondered if there were any other park specials hiding along the shore.

"Is that an overturned canoe?" Luce asked. She was apparently looking at the same thing I'd just focused on. "And . . . an alligator sunning next to it?

"Correct on both counts, my dear," I said. "I guess that definitively answers your earlier question, too."

The alligator opened his reptilian eyes and I got a good look at the beast's broad head. I continued to study the canoe behind him, wondering where it had come from on the little lake and why someone had left it overturned. A second later, I lowered my binos and used the corner of my shirt to wipe the lenses clean before raising the glasses back to my eyes.

Crap.

I wasn't seeing a smudge on my lens, after all.

That really was a man's hiking boot sticking out from beneath the end of the canoe.

A boot attached to a leg.

"I'm on vacation," I muttered. "I don't have time for this."

I laid my binoculars on my chest and turned to the group of birders beside me.

"Does anybody have cell phone reception out here? Because we need to call the park office and the police," I announced. "I think we've just added a dead man to today's park list."

Chapter Two

Thank you for your calm reaction when you realized you'd stumbled on another body," Luce said to me an hour or so later as we sat down at a table on the park's observation deck.

"I live to serve," I responded half-heartedly, "though acting as a dead person locator service is not one of my preferred job descriptions. Especially when I'm supposed to be on vacation," I added pointedly.

Luce patted my hand and continued.

"You did good, Bobby," she reassured me. "Given the ages of those birders, we may have had a couple of heart attacks on our hands if, instead, you'd yelled 'Call the cops! That's a dead body!' I mean, you and I have been down this road before, adding a dead man to our birding lists, but for these folks," she nodded at the elderly birders on the deck, "I'm sure it's a novel experience."

"I sure hope so," I muttered. "I'd hate to have to tell the next generation of birders that they should consider taking courses in forensics before they venture out into the field."

Although that was exactly what I'd started to think might be a good idea for myself.

With my body count now up to eight over the last few years, I was beginning to harbor the suspicion that maybe I was in the wrong business with my job as a high school counselor. The idea of making a career out of searching for bodies was not one that filled me with excitement, though I had to admit, I could generally depend on finding more avian rarities when I was trying to help the police solve a murder case than I ever could manage from my tiny broom closet of an office at Savage High School. If I had my career planning to do over again, I'd for sure look at double majoring in forensics and natural history.

Today's body, we learned, belonged to Birdy Johnson, Buzz Davis's birding buddy. After our 911 call to the local authorities, a flock of park personnel had descended on us at Alligator Lake, quickly followed by a swarm of the Weslaco city police and a squad of emergency vehicles. One of the park maintenance men had put a small boat in the water and ferried the police chief across the lake to the abandoned canoe. Upon their approach, the alligator slipped off into the water and sought a quieter shore for sunning, leaving them gator-less access to the scene.

Within minutes, the two men were back on our side of the lake with grim faces and an ID of the dead man.

"It's Birdy Johnson," the police chief announced to the assembled group. "I need all you folks who found the body to follow me back to the observation deck to give statements while our forensics team processes the scene. The rest of you need to clear out and give my guys space to do their jobs."

"What happened?" Rosalie, the volunteer naturalist we'd met on the deck, asked, tears brimming in her eyes and lips trembling. "I just saw him a few hours ago."

The chief held up his hands and motioned for us all to move back from the edge of the pond. "I can't share anything at this point. I need everyone out of here and on the deck."

I glanced around at what had grown into a small crowd of people in the aftermath of our unfortunate sighting.

Of the birders who'd been with us at Alligator Lake, the short woman with the straw hat and one of the men sat together at a table near the deck railing, quietly talking, while the remaining two fellows from our original group were listening to the instructions the local chief was giving to a crew of his deputies. Several detectives were comparing notes. Rosalie sat in a chair surrounded by other park personnel, saying nothing and wiping her eyes with a crumpled ivory handkerchief, while standing nearby, the park superintendent spoke quietly into her cell phone.

"I wonder if they've located Buzz Davis yet," I said. "As the last one to see his friend Birdy alive, I'm sure the chief and detectives will have plenty of questions for him."

Luce took a drink from the bottle of water she'd set on the table between us.

"I think I heard one of the park people saying he was going to go look for Buzz on the other side of the levee straight south from here," she said, wiping a line of perspiration from her forehead with the back of her hand. "I gathered it's a good spot for Sandpipers."

"It is," said one of the birders who'd just been hovering near the chief and deputies.

He was the white-haired birder we'd met at the lake. "I heard that you kids are visiting from Minnesota," he said, extending his hand to shake mine. "I'm Schooner Benedict from Duluth."

"I'm Bob White," I replied, "and this is my wife, Luce. We live in Savage on the southwestern side of the Twin Cities. Nice to meet you."

"I don't know that I'd call the circumstances 'nice,' given that we've got a dead birder on our hands," Schooner said, "but it's always good to see another Minnesotan down here. I'm a snow bird myself. A Winter Texan, we call it."

"So I've heard," I said. I glanced at his wildly flowered Hawaiian shirt and the beat-up straw hat that topped his snowy white hair.

Schooner laughed.

"I know. I look more like an escapee from a Caribbean cruise ship in this get-up, but I'm really a dyed-in-the-wool North Shore boy at heart. I grew up fishing Lake Superior and hiking along Hawk Ridge in Duluth before anyone called it Hawk Ridge. Heck, when I was six years old, the only people who even knew raptors were migrating along there were the local guys who used the hawks for target practice."

He took off his hat and held it over his heart, his face apologetic.

"I'm ashamed to say I shot at those hawks a few times, too, when I was a kid," he confessed. "What can I say? I was young and stupid. Appreciating the hawks and eagles and all the other birds came with maturity."

"Ah, don't let him fool you," a raspy male voice warned us.

The voice belonged to the man who had been sitting with the straw-hat woman at the table on the deck. He, too, had been in the group at Alligator Lake, I realized. Like the woman with the hat, he was short and round, but instead of straw, the hat on his head was a cloth ball cap with the White Sox baseball team logo on it.

"He's not nearly as mature as he should be, seeing how old he is," the newcomer said. "This guy's a dinosaur." He elbowed Schooner in the ribs. "I'm Paddy Mac. From the Irish side of Chicago."

He likewise wore a Hawaiian shirt, but whereas Schooner's shirt was loose and long over a thin torso, Paddy Mac's barely buttoned over his big belly. Fortunately, before I blurted out an impromptu fashion assessment, the third birder, the one with the head bandana and gray ponytail, who'd also been with us at the lake for our gruesome discovery, appeared behind Schooner and Paddy Mac. He looped his arms over the first two birders' shoulders.

"These clowns bothering you?" Bandana Man asked, leaning in towards me. He was a head taller than Schooner and Paddy Mac, his leathered face crinkled up by his grin. "I'm Gunnar," he said. "We're talking birds, aren't we?"

I had the unmistakable sensation that this must be what it felt like to have a trio of magpies corner you, especially when all three men immediately launched into an animated discussion without any prompting from me or Luce.

"Of course," Schooner said. "What else would we be talking about?"

"A dead body, maybe?" Gunnar suggested. "I don't know about you, but that was never on my bird list. Was it on yours?"

Schooner shook his head. "No. Can't say that it was."

"I ran across a Native American burial mound in North Carolina once when I was birding," Paddy Mac announced. "No one knew it was there until I found it."

"But you didn't see any actual bodies, did you?" Gunnar asked. "As in human remains?"

Paddy Mac gasped and melodramatically placed his hand at his throat.

"Ah, no," he said, his Irish brogue thick and exaggerated. "That would have been awful, me boy. Though I know a fella who found a skeleton when he was birding in Alaska," he said. "It was at the bottom of a ravine. He had to report it to the state patrol, but they said they couldn't get to it for a few days since it was such a long drive from their headquarters. They told the fella they doubted the skeleton would be going anywhere, anyway, so there was no rush in retrieving it."

"You're kidding, right?" Bandana Man Gunnar said, giving Paddy Mac a suspicious glance.

"No, it's the truth," Paddy insisted. "The birder found a skeleton, but he never found out how it got there."

"Speaking of which, what do you think happened to Birdy?" Schooner asked Gunnar. "Drug-runners or illegals?"

"Could have been a heart attack, for all we know," Gunnar answered. "It wouldn't be the first time one of us old birders kicked the bucket out in the field."

"Canoe," Schooner corrected him. "He kicked the canoe. It was lying on top of him. He must have tripped getting out of it and it flipped over on top of him. That's the only reason the gator didn't have him for lunch. Ooh," he cringed, "that would have been ugly."

"Would you fellows keep it down?"

I looked behind me to find the chief standing a foot or two away. I remembered from our brief introduction earlier when Luce and I gave him our statement about sighting the corpse that his name was Pacheco—Chief Juan Pacheco of the City of Weslaco, Texas. Like a large part of the population in the area, the chief was Hispanic, and I guessed he was in his mid-thirties, which put him in the minority age bracket with me and Luce, compared to the crowd of over-sixty-five-year-olds surrounding us on the park's deck.

Luce's earlier comment that we might have had a heart attack on our hands came back to me. As a high school counselor, I've taken training with our school nurse to keep my CPR certification up to date. I'd never considered that those same skills might be a pre-requisite for birding with Winter Texans; now that I thought about the age of most of the birders we'd met since arriving in the Rio Grande Valley, I could see where some emergency medical skills might come in handy.

Not that birding with older folks was anything unusual for me. I've been birding since I could hold a bird guide in my hand, which meant that I was typically the youngest birder by at least forty years in every group until I hit my own twenties.

In the last decade or so, however, I've noticed a marked increase in the numbers of younger people getting involved with birding, which is great for birds and birders everywhere, since appreciation of our natural spaces and species benefits everyone. At the same time, the ranks of birders have been expanding with the addition of new retirees as the baby boomers invest their interest (and money) in new hobbies. And since southern Texas was a magnet for retirees, it seemed like most of the folks Luce and I had met birding since we'd arrived were well into their senior discount days.

Gee, maybe there was a new occupational niche waiting for me here along the Rio Grande—I could lead birding trips with CPR available as an add-on option.

Then again . . . maybe not.

You know what they say—careful what you wish for, because you just might get it. I had to admit that, at this point in my life, counseling teenage drama queens still sounded pretty good to me compared to holding unexpected CPR sessions with senior birders.

Meanwhile, the chief had moved closer to our little clutch of conversation. He planted his feet apart and took a classic policeman's stance, folding impressively muscled arms over his uniformed chest.

It occurred to me that if a wrestling match had developed between him and the alligator, I would have bet on the chief winning. And if for some reason, he hadn't been able to throw the gator with a chokehold, the lawman did carry a mean-looking gun on his hip.

I hadn't noticed one on the alligator's.

"Rosalie is pretty upset as it is, gentlemen," Chief Pacheco told the three birders, nodding in the crying woman's direction. "In case you're unaware," he told them, "Rosalie and the deceased were very close, so I'd ask you to respect her grief and keep your comments to yourself."

"Sorry," Gunnar said.

"I wasn't thinking," Schooner chimed in.

Paddy Mac nodded. "We know Rosalie. I can't imagine how awful this is for her."

"And," Pacheco continued, "if you fellows want to share your theories with me, I'd be happy to have you come down to the station, and we can talk about it there, if need be. But I'm going to wait until I have the coroner's report before I start looking for suspects or speculating about what might have happened to Birdy. As far as I'm concerned, there was a very sad accident here this morning. Until my guy tells me different, I'm not jumping to any conclusions, and you guys shouldn't either. This is my department's business. Not yours."

"You're absolutely right," Paddy Mac said, nodding in agreement, his raspy tone turning contrite. "We beg your pardon, Chief. Our behavior has been inexcusable."

I caught Schooner and Gunnar exchanging a glance. It struck me that they were surprised at Paddy Mac's sudden change of demeanor, but neither man said a word about it. Instead, they shrugged, mumbled a few more quiet apologies to Pacheco, and then turned away to rejoin their birding comrades near the deck's railing.

That left Luce and me alone with the chief.

"You're free to leave," Chief Pacheco told us. "Thanks for your cooperation. And I'm sorry this happened on your vacation here. We've got a great destination for birdwatchers, and we're always happy to show off our Valley to visitors."

A commotion on the far side of the deck interrupted our conversation, and the three of us turned in the direction of the raised voices.

"What do you mean, Birdy's dead?"

I zeroed in on the tall fellow who was angrily stamping his big antler-topped walking stick on the deck, his bushy white eyebrows raised in alarm.

"It's your astronaut," I said to Luce. "Buzz. I guess the park employee located him after all."

"Where is he?" Buzz shouted. "I want to see him!"

Another loud wail came from Rosalie, the volunteer naturalist.

"This is not helping," Pacheco muttered and strode briskly away from us, towards Buzz.

"What is going on?" Buzz demanded, his voice only a degree less in volume.

From where we were standing, it looked like Buzz was using his walking stick to keep a park employee and a deputy at bay while they were trying to get the former astronaut to take a seat at a table on the deck. Out of the corner of my eye, I saw the park superintendent, a petite brown-haired woman, fall in behind Pacheco as he approached Buzz.

"She's no fool," Luce commented about the superintendent's move. "I'd want a brawny chief between me and that walking stick, too. That antler on top could be lethal given the right circumstances."

We watched Pacheco and the superintendent maneuver Buzz into a chair. Whatever they said to him calmed the man enough to convince him to lay down his walking stick and stop yelling. I could still hear Rosalie sobbing, and the crowd of birders and deputies continued to mill aimlessly around the park deck.

So much for another morning of successful vacation birding.

"Well," I said briskly to Luce. "I think we're done here, don't you? We got our Green Kingfisher and a Vermilion Flycatcher, so mission accomplished. How about lunch?"

Luce let out a heavy sigh. I saw her lovely blue eyes rest on Rosalie, who once again was wiping her eyes with the wadded-up handkerchief. Another uniformed park employee had taken the superintendent's place behind the bereaved naturalist, his hand resting on Rosalie's shoulder.

"This is so sad," Luce commented. She turned to face me and leaned in for a kiss. She smiled into my eyes and lightened her voice, too. "Yes, Mr. White, I think it's time we got out of here and got some lunch."

She looped her hand around my arm and we walked to the edge of the deck platform, but we came to a stop before stepping onto the brick-paved path that led back to the parking area.

"Oh, my gosh," she breathed.

"I see it, too," I said.

Perched almost directly in front of us on a branch of mesquite was a Great Kiskadee. While we'd already seen several of the native flycatchers during the last few days, this one was especially distinctive. Its yellow belly was almost incandescent amidst the branches, but it was its large head with its striking black-and-white face pattern that really caught our attention.

Especially since it was missing an eye on that head.

"It's the one-eyed Great Kiskadee," I said. "I thought Rosalie was joking earlier."

Luce studied the bird, which seemed perfectly content to sit for her inspection.

"I wonder what happened to it?" she mused. "How does a bird lose an eye like that?"

A reply to her question came from the other side of the mesquite.

"No one ever said Mother Nature was a push-over."

I could have sworn I knew the voice, but the spikey fronds of a Sabal Palm blocked a clear view of the person climbing out of the tangle of brush and trees towards us. I caught a glimpse of a flannel plaid shirt and bright red suspenders just as the visually impaired Great Kiskadee flew away.

"In fact, sometimes she can be downright nasty, you know."

The man ducked his head to avoid the last branches of mesquite and emerged onto the brick pathway. His big belly preceded him.

I blinked, just to be sure I wasn't imagining the familiar face above it.

"Crazy Eddie?" I said. "What in the world are you doing here?"

My old friend Eddie Edvarg beamed us a big grin through his full white beard. A Norwegian by birth and Minnesotan by residency, Eddie had won an enormous lottery many years ago and secluded himself and his wife on a big spread north of Duluth, which he rarely left. The only times I now ran into Eddie were when he'd been enticed by someone to take on a high-tech, electronics project that had captured his interest. The man was an absolute genius when it came to gizmos.

Even if he did look like a Santa with his white beard and round belly.

"I was pretty sure I heard a Bob White over here," Eddie laughed.

"Eddie, what a nice surprise!" Luce said, throwing her arms around him for a hug.

Over my wife's shoulder, my old buddy gave me a wink.

"So you went and married this kid, huh?" he asked Luce. "Even though he's not Norwegian? Well, you could have done worse, I suppose. He could have been a full-blooded Swede. This still calls for a drink."

He began patting his plaid shirt and baggy khaki pants, obviously looking for the small bottle of Aquavit, the traditional Norwegian liquor, that he always carried. I remembered the first time Luce met Eddie when we'd been looking for Boreal Owls up in his neck of the Superior Forest—she thought he was Santa on an ATV—and he'd been enchanted by my wife's Norwegian heritage, not to mention her striking Nordic looks. Despite our decade-long friendship begun when we worked together one summer tracking moose for the Minnesota Department of Natural Resources, Eddie never missed an opportunity to give me a hard time about my mother's Swedish background. I think he felt obligated to keep alive the traditional not-always-friendly rivalry between Norway and Sweden.

Even though he was as American as I was.

"Now where did that bottle go?" Eddie muttered, hunting methodically through his pockets. "Cripes, where did I leave it?"

"So what are you doing here?" I asked him again.

He gave up his search for the Aquavit and folded his arms over the top of his stomach.

"This and that," he said. "The wife went with her book club on a Caribbean cruise with some author who writes romance novels. I said 'No way I'm joining you for that one, honey,' and decided I'd visit some old friends down here while she's out on the water drinking little umbrella drinks and talking about unrequited love and unbridled passion."

I gave Eddie an expectant stare.

"What?" he said, feigning innocence. "You like those books? Why, Bob, I never knew."

Luce laughed.

"Cough it up, Eddie," I said. "I know you. You're here working, aren't you? Robotics or surveillance?"

He pursed his lips and squinted up at me.

"All right," he conceded, "there was a little bitty job I thought I'd check out here as a favor to an old friend."

"I knew it," I said. "Who's the friend?"

"What's the job?" Luce asked.

Eddie grinned. "You two practice that?" He pointed at me, then at Luce. "That one-two thing? Finishing each other's thoughts? How long have you been married?"

A shout rose behind me.

"There he is!"

I turned to see Rosalie, our grieving naturalist, walking towards us, accompanied by Chief Pacheco. Rosalie still clutched a handkerchief in her hand, holding it against her lips, and the chief looked grim.

I wondered what they wanted.

As it turned out, it wasn't me.

"Are you Eddie Edvarg?" the chief barked out, directing his attention to Eddie.

"Yes, sir," Eddie responded. "How can I help you?"

Pacheco came to a stop in front of us.

"Excuse me, folks, but I need to speak with Mr. Edvarg."

He turned to Eddie. "Are you the special contractor who's been testing the new surveillance sensors down at the river?" His words came out more as an accusation than a question.

Eddie paused a moment to look the chief over. I guessed he was as startled as I was at the chief's confrontational tone.

"I am."

Pacheco gestured back towards the park deck. "Then you'll please come with me to answer a few questions," he said.

It was a command, not a request.

Eddie squinted at the chief, sizing him up.

Compared to Eddie's barely five-foot frame, I'd say 'up' was the operational word there, since Pacheco matched my own six-foot three-inch height. Besides which, the chief was a lot more muscled than my old friend, not to mention he was armed with a service revolver. Wisely, Eddie decided to go peacefully.

"Okay," he told the officer, "Lead the way."

Luce and I remained standing with Rosalie while the two men returned to the park deck.

"You know Eddie?" Rosalie asked me.

"He's an old friend," I said.

"You know why he is here?"

I shook my head. "We were just asking him, but we didn't get the answer."

Rosalie dabbed carefully at her eyes.

"He's working with the U.S. Customs and Border Patrol," she informed us. "Something to do with the new sensors to discourage illegal border crossings."

"That sounds like Eddie," I commented. "He loves that kind of work."

"He had talked with Birdy about it," she said, her voice catching. "And Birdy told me we would have to keep an eye on Eddie, for everyone's sake."

She looked back in the direction where the chief had taken Eddie.

"And now . . . now Birdy is dead," she sniffed, her eyes brimming with tears.

"So the chief wants to question Eddie about Birdy?" Luce asked.

Rosalie nodded, her lips trembling. "Yes," she said, barely above a whisper. "I overheard one of the deputies. He said he found a small empty bottle of some kind of drink near the body. Schooner and Gunnar overheard him, too. They told me it was a special liquor from Minnesota."

"Oh, no," Luce breathed beside me.

I felt my stomach roll in dread.

"The liquor," I said, "was it called Aquavit?"

Rosalie looked at me suspiciously.

"Yes." She nodded. "That was the name. How do you know that?"

"Just a wild guess," I said, my stomach in complete free fall.

"Oh, no," Luce repeated.

I took my wife's hand in mine and gave it a reassuring squeeze.

"On second thought, maybe we aren't done here, yet," I told her, starting to lead the way back to the park deck. "I don't know what kind of mischief Eddie's gotten himself into, but I know for a fact he's not a killer."

At least, I really hoped not.

Don't you just hate it when you're wrong?

Chapter Three

As it turned out, though, Luce and I were done with Estero Llano Grande State Park for the day. Just as we stepped back on the park deck, Eddie and the chief passed us, walking in the opposite direction towards the park's entrance and parking lot.

"I'm taking a ride with the chief here to the police station," Eddie called back to us. "Don't worry. I'm just going to give him my statement. Then I'll ring your cellphone. See if we can have dinner."

Luce and I watched the two men follow the brick path until they veered out of our sight. I hadn't spotted any cuffs on Eddie, so I figured he was going along willingly in order to fully cooperate with the chief's investigation. No need to antagonize the local law if you didn't have to, right?

Especially if it was your bottle of Minnesota Aquavit found near a fresh corpse.

In Texas.

Where you were working on a special project.

What a coincidence.

"The chief obviously knew that someone was working with the surveillance system," Luce observed, still looking in the direction the men had gone. "But he clearly hadn't met Eddie yet."

She turned to face me. "Although if Eddie is working with the Border Patrol, I suppose that might be a different agency than the chief's department. I hope there isn't bad blood between the two groups, but I got the impression the chief wasn't too keen on the project Eddie's involved with."

I'd noticed the same thing, as I'm sure Eddie had, too, judging from the way he'd reacted to the chief's initial greeting.

"I expect it's probably a jurisdictional thing," I surmised. "Government agencies and local police departments seem to be easily offended when they bump into each other on cases, even though everybody's on the same team." I paused. "Or at least, they're supposed to be on the same team."

Luce drew her sunglasses out of her backpack and slipped them on. "Let's go get lunch," she said. "We're not going to be hearing from Eddie for a couple of hours, anyway."

"Lunch it is, then," I agreed. "Fat Daddy's Barbeque, here we come."

Less than ten minutes later, I was signaling a left turn off the highway into the parking lot of Fat Daddy's. We'd passed the restaurant on our way to Estero Llano, and while the place had been empty at the earlier hour, there was now a line of people crowding into the door, and a parking lot filled with random rows of cars.

I'd gotten the tip to eat there from Birdchick, one of my birding colleagues back home in Minnesota, when I told her Luce and I were heading to McAllen, Texas, she said we had to try the barbeque at Fat Daddy's in Weslaco. Birdchick travels all over the world birding, so when she recommends an eating spot, you can be sure it's good. Of course, the fact that Fat Daddy's was also conveniently located so close to the entrance to Estero Llano made it an easy choice for a meal for anyone visiting the park.

I just hadn't expected that everyone from the park, and the surrounding county, it seemed, would want to be eating there at the same time as us.

"What do you think?" I asked Luce as I tried to find a parking spot amid the jumble of cars. "Shall we go somewhere else less crowded?"

"Absolutely not," she replied. "Most of the car license plates are from here, which means the locals love it. That's the kind of restaurant we want. And I've had this craving for barbeque ever since we left Minnesota," she added, pointing at a car that was backing out of the lot in a cloud of dust. "There's our spot."

I made a tight turn into the space, and after we got out of the car, we waited for another two cars to pass by before we could head to the entrance to Fat Daddy's.

"It's a fifteen-minute wait," the young hostess told me when I angled my way through the waiting crowd to her noisy station inside the old clapboard building. The interior walls were paneled in wood and covered with memorabilia: autographed photos, longhorn skulls, framed local news articles, flags, and sports jerseys. Every table was occupied, and a team of waitresses scurried around the room, delivering plates of pulled pork sandwiches and steaming barbequed chicken.

"I think this might be Texas barbeque heaven," Luce said when I rejoined her at the end of the line of customers that wound out the front door. "It sure smells like it is."

I had to agree. I would have said something to that effect, but my mouth was too busy salivating in anticipation. I could almost taste the tangy sauced beef and pork ribs thanks to the thick aromas that had filled the dining room inside.

Four soldiers in fatigues fell in line behind us. I guessed they were in their early twenties, and I noticed they all had an American flag patch on their upper right arms.

"Hey, guys," I said. "Thanks for your service."

The soldier nearest me smiled. "You're welcome," he replied.

"Is there a military base near here?" Luce asked.

"Army National Guard, ma'am," said another of the soldiers. "We've got an armory here in the city of Weslaco."

I noticed that his name tape read *Pacheco*.

"We just met a chief named Pacheco out at Estero Llano," I commented. "No possibility you're related, I suppose?"

The young Guardsman laughed. "As a matter of fact, he's my cousin. Two or three times removed—I can never remember which it is, since we've got so many cousins in the Valley. He was sort of my hero growing up," he explained, "so I followed him into the Guard when I was old enough."

His companions made clucking sounds, and one of them piped up, "Poor little boy. You were the *pollo chiquito* in the henhouse."

Pacheco pretended to punch his friend. "Hey, I grew up to be the *gallo*! Not my fault my parents had six daughters and only one son."

The men all laughed.

The young Guardsman resumed his conversation with me and Luce.

"But my cousin, the chief, went into local law enforcement when his eight years were up," he went on. "He said he wanted to clean up this border zone, but I think he couldn't bring himself to leave all the relatives. A lot of us here have family on both sides of the border."

He pointed at his own uniformed chest. "As for me, I'm heading to California when I'm done, and I'm not looking back."

One of his comrades gave him a friendly shove on the shoulder. "Yeah, right. And where will that leave your Pearlita, the Citrus Queen? Home all alone in Mission?"

Mission was one of the cities we'd visited in the last few days. Surrounded by citrus groves, it was the local capital of Texas fruit-growers, and the site of the annual Citrus Festival, which happened to be slated during our week of vacation. In honor of the celebration, Luce and I had both ordered our first slices of grapefruit pie for dessert the night before.

The other two soldiers laughed while Pacheco grinned.

"I'll keep your Pearlita company!" the guardsman standing next to me eagerly offered.

"You wish!" Pacheco shot back, joining in the laughter.

"Pacheco's girlfriend is this year's Citrus Queen," one of the quartet explained. "She'll be in the festival parade on Saturday, riding the float for the Valley's citrus growers. She'll be the one holding the big grapefruits," he added, holding his hands at chest level and winking suggestively at his comrades.

"Hey!" Pacheco objected indignantly, even as his buddies burst into another round of laughter. "Show some respect!"

"White, party of two?"

I turned to see our hostess waiting for us with two menus.

"Was that fifteen minutes?" I asked Luce as we followed the hostess to our table in the covered porch dining area of Fat Daddy's. We took our seats at a small table covered with a cheerful red-and-white-checkered plastic cloth. A roll of paper towels sat on its end in the middle of the plastic.

"This is serious barbeque," Luce said, then dove into studying the menu.

I glanced around the porch. A big American flag hung on one end of the room, and I noted that we were one of only two tables not occupied by soldiers in fatigues. Fat Daddy's was clearly the lunching establishment of choice for the local Guardsmen, and as I watched a nimble young waitress set down a loaded tray of heaping portions of barbequed chicken and pork, I could understand why. Not only did the food smell terrific, but there was plenty of it, and after a morning of birding gone bad, I was more than ready to turn my attention to some good, old-fashioned comfort food.

Our waitress came over to the table, and Luce and I both ordered the pulled pork sandwich with a side of coleslaw and potato salad. As we sipped on our iced teas, I wondered how Eddie's conversation with the chief was going. I didn't want to even speculate how his trademark bottle of Aquavit might have ended up near a dead man, but unless my old friend had a rock-solid alibi for his morning, I doubted that the chief was going to write off Eddie as a prime suspect in the murder of Birdy Johnson. Just to be sure I hadn't missed any calls from Eddie amid the surrounding din of happy diners, I took out my cell phone to check.

Nope.

No calls.

Was that a good or bad thing?

"Bobby, have you ever heard anything about a Space X program?"

Luce's question prompted me to put my phone away and turn my attention in her direction. She was pointing at a framed news article that hung on the wall behind our table. The headline was about the Citrus Festival Parade's Grand Marshals from the year before, and below it was a photograph of two men waving from the platform of a parade float that looked like it was a rocket ship made of oranges.

Something about one of the men in the picture made me think I'd seen his face before. I peered at the grainy photo, trying to place the man.

"It's Buzz Davis," Luce said, doing her usual trick of reading my mind. "And the caption reads 'Buzz Davis and Birdy Johnson are giving Rio Grande Valley residents something besides citrus to celebrate this year. The two men will be welcoming the first load of passengers on the historic first flight that will change the Valley forever. More about Space X on page 5.'"

She waited for me to look away from the newspaper clipping and back at her.

"That's Birdy Johnson with Buzz," she said. "That's the man we found dead in the park."

I glanced back at the framed newsprint. "Not that I want to rain on their parade, but for some reason, I don't think that rockets made from oranges are going to make it as the next generation of space vehicles."

Luce reached across the table and smacked me on the shoulder.

"Ow!"

"I'm trying to be serious here," she reprimanded me.

"So am I!" I protested. "I wouldn't buy stock in some company making rockets out of oranges."

I put up my hands to ward off another smack from my wife.

"No, I don't know anything about a Space X, to answer your question," I said. "And whoever mounted this clipping didn't considerately include page 5, so I guess we're out of luck."

At that moment, our waitress returned with our baskets of lunch and laid them in front of us.

"Thank you," I told the young woman. She threw me a quick smile and hustled away to another table. I looked at Luce across the table from me. "We are not, however, out of food. Dig in, my dear."

"Hey, Minnesota!"

I turned to look in the direction of the voice that rose above the din of the porch and recognized our three magpies from the park—Schooner, Gunnar, and Paddy Mac. I lifted a hand in a brief wave, and by the time I got my fingers back on my pulled pork sandwich, the men had crossed the room and were standing next to our table.

"We won't keep you from your lunch," Schooner said. "You obviously know the right birders if you found this place already—the barbeque's to die for."

He abruptly stopped talking and scrubbed his hand over his face.

"Sorry," he added. "Given the circumstances, that was a pretty thoughtless comment."

Paddy Mac punched Schooner in the arm. "Thoughtless? More like oblivious. Where is your sense of decorum, man?"

"We want to recruit you," Gunnar said, ignoring his companions' banter. "If you folks are going to be here a few more days, we are in desperate need of some help, and us birders have got to flock together, right?"

"What kind of help?" Luce asked, pausing between bites of her sandwich.

"Night work," Paddy Mac said. He looked both ways as if checking to see who might be within earshot, then leaned toward me and loudly whispered, "We've got a deadline."

This time, it was Schooner punching Paddy Mac in the shoulder. "Now who's being oblivious?"

"Sorry," Paddy Mac smiled sheepishly. "Not thinking."

"Look," Gunnar said. "You help us out, and we'll help you. We've got some ideas about how to get your friend Eddie cleared with the chief."

I looked at each of the men in turn.

"What do we have to do?"

Paddy Mac leaned in to whisper in my ear.

"We're members of the MOB, and we've got a job for you, Minnesota."

Chapter Four

I pulled back to look at Paddy Mac. Without his Sox ball cap on, Paddy's bald head looked pale and fragile, but his scruffy beard had hints of dull red mixed in with an iron gray. Though we'd spoken a few times earlier in the morning, I only now noticed the flesh-colored plastic piece of a hearing aid peeking around the top edge of his right ear.

"You can't fool me," I said, being sure to speak a bit more loudly than my normal volume. "You're Irish, not Italian." I pointed at Schooner. "And my guess is you've got some Norseman in you seeing as you're from Duluth."

I turned to Gunnar.

"Which leaves you. I could believe you're a grandfather, but a Godfather?" I tapped the side of my head and nodded at his own bandana-wrapped skull. "For some reason, I don't think so."

The three men chuckled.

"You got us pegged, Minnesota," Gunnar said. "Not an Italian in the bunch. We're talking MOB—as in McAllen's Older Birders. It's the name of the birding club down here. The local senior citizens hold the fort down through the summers, but once it's winter, we snowbirds show up to pick up the slack. It's a big group. Your buddy Eddie signed on with us a couple weeks ago. He's part of the family now."

"So what's the job you want me to do?"

Paddy Mac gripped my shoulder. "We got a float to finish for the Citrus Parade, and without Birdy—may he rest in peace—and maybe Eddie, if he's in jail, we need all the help we can get to have that float ready to roll day after tomorrow. Can you help us out?"

He looked pleadingly at me, then at Luce. "You're too young for the MOB, but we could sure use the help."

Luce ripped a paper towel from the roll on the table and wiped a smear of barbeque sauce from her chin. "What do you think, Minnesota?" she asked me, emphasizing my new nickname. "Want to roll in some citrus?"

I could feel her toe nudging my shin underneath the table as I regarded her mischievous grin. I had the clear impression she wasn't thinking about a parade entry at all.

I returned her invitation with a grin of my own. "Love to," I challenged her.

I turned to our three magpies. "Tell us where and when, and we'll be there."

Paddy Mac ripped off a corner of paper towel from our roll and jotted down an address for me, just as our waitress appeared behind Gunnar to take the men to their table on the opposite side of the enclosed porch. I pocketed the address with a pledge to see them later, and Luce and I returned to our meals.

"Schooner was right," Luce said as we waited for our check a half-hour later. "This barbeque is to die for."

I was about to agree with her assessment of our lunch when my cell phone chirped in my pocket. I checked the caller ID and saw that it was Eddie.

"Do you mind if I answer?" I asked Luce. We'd agreed on our drive south to Texas to avoid using our cell phones during meals, but I thought this warranted an exception. "It's our perhaps-in-jail bird."

"Take it," she said. "I'm going to go use the ladies' room."

I accepted the call and watched Luce wind her way through the crowded tables to the restrooms located near the front door. I saw more than one Guardsman's head turn her way as she passed. Amid the sea of dark-haired women lunching at Fat Daddy's, my wife's blonde hair stood out like a beacon. Coupled with her own six feet of height, I didn't doubt her Scandinavian looks were a novelty to many of the soldiers enjoying their sandwiches at the restaurant.

In fact, I was sure the young Guardsmen we'd met while waiting for our table had been more than a little awed by Luce, even though their conversation focused on the Citrus Queen girlfriend of one of the men.

Pacheco, I remembered. He was related to the chief who'd taken Eddie into the station.

"Eddie," I said into my phone. "Please tell me this isn't the one phone call you're allowed when you get arrested."

At the other end of the connection Eddie laughed.

"No, Bob. I'm not in the slammer yet." He paused a moment and his voice lost some of its usual joviality. "But I also don't know if I'm completely absolved of any wrongdoing, either. My Aquavit showing up beside Birdy is . . . problematic . . . for lack of a better word."

I waited for him to continue, but the phone was quiet in my hand.

"What can I do, Eddie?" I asked him. "You need a ride back to Estero Llano?"

"No, I'm good. The chief is giving me a lift back. He's got more work to do out there. Where are you and Luce headed? Maybe we could meet up for dinner later."

My eyes roamed over the room still filled with diners, and I happened to catch a glimpse of the soldier named Pacheco as he and his pals paid their bill at the cashier's desk.

"We're going to visit the Valley Nature Center in Weslaco," I told him. "It's not too far from here, and I heard they have a nice little sanctuary that attracts some great birds. Hey, Eddie," I said, "tell the chief we met his second or third or something cousin at Fat Daddy's—a young Guardsman whose girlfriend is the Citrus Queen. Apparently the chief was in the National Guard himself at some point."

I saw Luce emerge from the hallway that led to the restrooms. As she passed by the cashier's desk, she turned her head to say something to the departing Guardsmen and they responded with smiles and waves as they went out the door.

"I'm staying at the Alamo Inn in Alamo," Eddie said in my ear. "Swing that way after you see the nature center, and we'll get an early dinner."

"Sounds like a plan," I replied, watching my wife approach our table. "Hey, Eddie," I said again, "looks like Luce and I are going to be joining you for some float-building tonight, too. We got recruited by the MOB."

"You did?" He sounded surprised. "Well, that should make for an interesting evening, then. I'll have a chance to introduce you to all the usual suspects. Literally," he added.

Something about his tone chilled me despite the filled room of noisy diners and the heat I could feel emanating from the heaped plates of food as the waitresses continued to distribute hot baskets of barbeque around me. Luce pulled out her chair and sat down again, her eyes on my face.

"Still Eddie?" she quietly asked.

I nodded. "Why do I get the feeling you're not telling me something?" I said to Eddie, probing for the reason for his particular choice of those last words. "Did the chief tell you not to leave town?"

"Not exactly," Eddie admitted. "In fact, he hinted that he might want me to help him out with his investigation."

I briefly considered what Eddie was saying. Based on my own experience of working with police, a death was only an 'investigation' when there were questions about its cause. And that meant there had to be some clear evidence from the get-go to indicate that the death was not a result of natural causes. Seeing a dead body lying partially covered by a canoe wasn't, as far as I knew, conclusive proof foul play was involved.

Although, I have to admit, the idea that someone in the throes of a heart attack or lung failure or massive spontaneous stroke would have the strength or inclination to flip a big canoe over on top of himself didn't strike me as a common reaction to imminent death.

Actually, it didn't strike me as a common reaction to anything. Canoes are heavy. Awkward. No one I knew used canoes as make-shift housing, especially if alligators were in the vicinity.

Which really made me wonder what the chief had found when he and the park maintenance guy had rowed across the lake to check out the overturned canoe and dead body.

Besides the bottle of Eddie's Aquavit he recovered, that is.

Eddie's voice broke into my sidetracked train of thought.

"I said 'usual suspects,' Bob, because Birdy Johnson's death was not an accident," Eddie confirmed in answer to my unasked question. "And Chief Pacheco thinks there's a good chance the killer might be a member of the MOB."

The faces of the three magpies appeared in my head. They did-n't strike me as murderers. A comedy troupe, maybe, but cold-blooded killers?

Not a chance.

"So what's the chief got for a lead in that direction, Eddie?"

He told me and ended the call.

"What is it?" Luce asked, a trace of alarm in her voice.

Her question surprised me. Like I already mentioned, Luce is a mind reader; she knows what I'm thinking almost as soon as I do, a talent she seemed to develop from the first day we met, crammed into the back of a tiny car during a birding group weekend in north-western Minnesota. Since then, she's sharpened that skill to the point where now, I sometimes think she knows what I'm going to be thinking *before* I even think it.

"You're slipping," I said. "Must be because you're on vacation, right?"

She gave me a light kick in my left shin under the table.

"Ow."

Lunch was turning out a lot rougher than I had expected. Texas must have been bringing out my wife's feisty side.

I reached down and rubbed my leg. Luce tried to hide the smirk on her face, but I caught it.

"I take it back," I apologized. "It must have been a momentary lapse . . . on my part," I added. "Chief Pacheco found a few things besides Eddie's Aquavit near Birdy's body," I answered her question. "One was a cracked skull, which belonged to Birdy."

Luce grimaced.

"And the other was a bird checklist from Estero Llano, with an address scrawled on it, but it wasn't in Birdy's handwriting, apparently."

I pulled from my pocket the scrap of paper that Paddy Mac had handed me.

"This address," I said. "I guess that means there's a chance we might be nailing grapefruit and oranges to a parade float tonight with a killer beside us."

Luce locked her blue eyes on mine.

"Then I get dibs on the nail gun," she said. "I know you don't like guns, but I don't have that problem, and I'm not going in unarmed."

Feisty?

Make that dangerous. Luce grew up hunting with her dad in the woods every year during deer hunting season in Minnesota. Believe me, the woman was an eagle-eye with a rifle. I reminded myself not to tease her if I saw a nail gun in her hands later on in the day. I really didn't need to know how far it could shoot. Two "ows" were plenty for the day.

I picked up the check our waitress had left on the table and ushered my sharp-shooter wife to the cashier's desk, which was mobbed with exiting diners paying their bills.

As I stood in line, I saw on the wall near the cash register another framed news clipping with "SpaceX" in the headline. The article was a reprint from an Internet site called rt.com, and it featured a photo of a sleek spacecraft. I read aloud what I could see.

"'SpaceX has announced it will build the world's first commercial launch pad for orbital rockets in the south of Texas. The facility, which is expected to drag the area out of an economic hole, might become operational in 2016.'"

"Man, would I love to get a ride on that bird," said a voice behind me.

I turned to see another group of uniformed National Guardsmen behind me in the check-out line. The one who had spoken gave me a nod of acknowledgment.

"They've already got the first passenger flight booked," the man commented, raising his voice to carry to me over the din of the restaurant, "and there's a waiting list to get on it, if you can afford the price. Can you imagine? Riding on the first commercial rocket to go for a spin in space. That would be something to write home about."

One of the soldier's companions jostled against his shoulder. "What? Fat Daddy's isn't enough for you to write home about? We are talking good barbeque here. You're not going to find that in outer space."

The men laughed together, and I turned back to find myself facing the cashier. I paid our bill and joined Luce where she was waiting by the door that led out to the parking lot.

"That solves the SpaceX mystery," I told her. "It's a commercial space launch base that's going to be built somewhere around here. Makes sense then that Buzz Davis was involved with it, I guess. He was an astronaut. A space base would probably be right up his alley. Or maybe I should say up his quadrant—isn't that how they locate places in space?"

Luce shook her head and ignored my question. "I wonder what Birdy's connection was? Since he and Buzz were friends, and they were both in that parade picture from last year, they must have been working together on SpaceX."

We got into the car, which was warm and toasty from the Texas sun.

"Oh, man," I breathed as I put the key in the ignition. "This is the way I want to spend January. Warm and birding in a t-shirt. Really, I think I could live happily ever after without ever again putting on another down parka and thermal underwear."

Luce didn't say anything in reply, so I gave her a curious glance. She was gazing out the front windshield. I followed her line of sight to a stand of trees just beyond the parking lot.

"It's the one-eyed Great Kiskadee," she said.

I watched it for a moment before it spread its wings and flew away. At the same moment, our friends from the MOB walked out of Fat Daddy's and headed for their own vehicle in the lot.

A murderer in the McAllen Older Birders club?

I was having a hard time picturing any senior citizen cracking someone's skull, but I had to admit, I was no stranger to finding the unusual. In fact, I'd made my birding reputation in Minnesota by finding uncommon birds all over the place, sometimes by sheer determination and patience alone.

But a seventy-something murderer?

I figured that was about as likely as . . .

My eyes drifted back to where the one-eyed Great Kiskadee had perched on the edge of the lot.

Now that I thought about it, the unusual could just as easily be sitting right in front of our faces, couldn't it?

Chapter Five

About an hour later, I was counting Plain Chachalacas as they roamed around on the ground in front of us in the bird feeding viewing area of the Valley Nature Center in Weslaco, Texas. As members of the Galliformes order of birds, a crowd of Chachalacas might remind you of a farmyard flock of fowl with their noisy socializing and lack of concern about humans lurking nearby. If you watched the classic adventure film *Jurassic Park* when you were a kid, like I did, however, a flock of Chachalacas might also remind you of a pack of little velociraptors.

But without the suspenseful soundtrack in the background or the digitally-enhanced murderous gleam in their eyes.

Really, we're talking hens here, not flesh-rending dinosaurs.

Their common name is actually a rough approximation of their call—four notes that sound like *cha-cha-lac-a*. Not exactly terrifying, but certainly distinctive enough to catch your attention. After another moment or two of watching the birds, I spotted the individual in the flock that the nature center's greeter had told us about: a piebald Plain Chachalaca. Typically, the birds are brown in color, but this one was the exception, making it stand out among its peers.

"Oops," I commented to Luce. "I bet that one's mama had some explaining to do to its daddy."

"You are such an idiot," she said, giving me the evil eye.

I laughed and pulled her close for a kiss. "But you love me for it, don't you?"

"Ah, excuse me, sir?"

A pretty young woman seemed to materialize out of the scrub along one side of the bird viewing area. Dressed in an olive green shirt and pants, she had blended right into the scenery. Unlike the piebald Chachalaca, her coloration had hidden her well.

I released my wife and gave the young woman my attention instead.

"Yes?"

She stepped over a pile of branches and came closer to where we stood. Now that I could see her better, I guessed she was in her late teens or maybe early twenties. Her dark hair was pulled back into a sleek braid that disappeared down her back and the nature center's logo was on her shirt. I read her nametag: Pearl Garcia.

"Color abnormalities can happen in any species," she informed me. "Albinos, for example, are probably the color abnormality most familiar to people. The fact is that there are three main types of pigments found in feathers, and some birds have one kind of pigment, and others have another kind. Then, when an individual bird has one of those pigments missing or too dominant, you get a color variation from the norm."

She pointed in the direction the piebald bird had scurried.

"Like that Chachalaca," she said.

"Very good," I complimented her. "Are you a birder, or is that just information all the employees here are required to know?"

The young woman smiled. "I'm a volunteer here and a birder," she told me. "My grandmother made sure I memorized the names of the birds in her garden when I was a little girl. Before long, I was memorizing their vocalizations, too. I teach a class here to help people learn to bird by ear."

Luce put her arm around my shoulder. "That's one of this guy's many charms," she told Pearl. "He's an expert at birding by ear."

Pearl's cheekbones reddened slightly. "And here I'm lecturing you about birds. I'm sorry. I meet so many people here at the center who are just beginning to take an interest in birds, I just assumed when you made the comment about the piebald . . ." she shrugged her shoulders in apology.

"I'm Bob White," I said, hoping to diffuse her embarrassment.

She cocked her head and looked at me doubtfully. Luce laughed.

"No, really," I assured the young birder. "That's my name."

"And I'm Luce. His wife," Luce introduced herself. "We're from Minnesota, and we're spending a week here in the Lower Rio Grande Valley to get some sunshine and new birds on our life lists."

"Don't forget the lemons," I reminded her. I turned to Pearl. "My wife is an amazing chef, and she says there is nothing better than fresh citrus off the tree."

Pearl smiled, her brown eyes widening. "Then you have to come for the Citrus Festival Parade on Saturday. The main street in Mission is closed off for it, and people line the streets to watch. Some people come hours early to get a good seat, in fact."

"Sounds like a pretty big deal," I commented.

"Oh, it is!" she enthused. "There are bands, and horses, and floats all decorated with citrus fruit. And the street food is amazing! You have to try the chile and cheese *gorditas*—everyone says they're never better than the ones you can buy at the parade carts. The whole town comes out."

A rapping sound interrupted Pearl's parade pitch. In almost perfect synchrony, our three heads turned toward the noise in the trees.

"Up about twenty feet," Pearl said, pointing at the bird. "A Golden-fronted Woodpecker. We have quite a few here at the nature center."

"Nice view of him," I said. "I can see his red cap."

"He looks a lot like our Red-bellied Woodpecker at home," Luce noted. "They've both got the black-and-white barred back and they're about the same size. But there's no mistaking this guy with that bright gold nape."

"Golden-fronted Woodpeckers are native to Mexico and Central America," Pearl added. "The farthest north you might see them are in Oklahoma. The Lower Rio Grande Valley is where the Mississippi and Central flyways converge, you know, which is why our bird species are so plentiful."

"Really?" I said. "Imagine that."

Luce gave me a jab with her elbow. I threw her a wink.

"Have you walked all our trails here?" Pearl asked. "It's really only about a mile of walking, but in five acres, we have all the native habitats of the Lower Rio Grande Valley. We probably have hundreds of birds and butterflies, too."

As if to prove the accuracy of her words, a Black-crested Titmouse flitted past us into the mesquite and thorn scrub that bordered one side of the viewing area just as a Buff-bellied Hummingbird flew in to draw nectar from a native plant. At the same time, a Red-bordered Pixie butterfly floated across the open space to land on a branch not far from Pearl's shoulder.

"We skipped the bog pond," I told our young birder. "And we have plenty of wetlands back home, so we focused on the Cactus and Resaca Trails."

"My grandmother says our Resaca Trail is very authentic with the plants we've got growing in there," Pearl told us. "She grew up in Mexico, just south of Brownsville, where the coastal plain and dry river channels created rich farmlands. She worked in the fields when she was a kid. Every day, she'd tell me, she would rise very early, while it was still dark, to go out to the fields to help her parents pick produce all day. She hated it. So when she came to live in Texas, she was thrilled to go to school instead of into the fields to pick."

Pearl gave us a big smile. "And she told me that story every time I complained about going to school. She'd shake her finger at me and say, '*Lo tienes muy bien aqui, Pearlita. Quedate en la escuela, y no te quejas.*' That means, 'You have it so good here, Pearlita. No complaining. Go to school.'"

She checked the slim gold watch on her wrist and offered us another smile. "And now I have to go do that. I've got a late afternoon class at South Texas College over in McAllen. I'm planning to be an electrical engineer. You two enjoy your time here. It was nice to meet you."

Luce and I bid Pearl goodbye and then watched her disappear back into the scrub.

"Nice kid," I said.

"She's not a kid," Luce corrected me. "She's a young woman. And it sounds like she's pretty attached to her grandmother."

"Who taught her to look at the birds," I reminded her.

"And to stay in school," Luce countered. "I'd say that makes for a pretty awesome grandmother. I wonder if she lives with Pearl? It seems like there are a lot of multi-generational households in this area."

I knew from my own experience counseling our Latino students at Savage High School that extended families living together under one roof was a fairly common cultural practice. Like Pearl, those students benefitted greatly from the influence of their elders, not the least being the encouragement my students received to do well in school. I totally believed that, if I could assign a conscientious, hard-working grandparent to mentor every student I had, Latino or any other ethnic group, including Caucasian, I'd be dealing with a lot fewer problem children.

"Wherever she lives," I said, "Pearl's grandma rates in my book."

I checked my own watch for the time. "I think we should go check out the Alamo Inn where Eddie's staying. He said he'd be ready for an early dinner."

We walked the Butterfly Trail, lined with a variety of native trees and bushes, back to the Visitor's Center, where the sound of sobbing greeted us as soon as we entered the building. A quick scan of the lobby revealed a small clutch of women huddled around the source of the crying near the receptionist's desk. I tried to avert my eyes and leave the group to its privacy, but just because I was on vacation from my counseling job didn't mean I'd been able to leave all my counseling instincts back at home in Minnesota.

I looked at the huddle.

The next thing I knew, my eyes were locked in surprised mutual recognition with the gaze of Rosalie, the volunteer naturalist and very upset friend of the deceased Birdy Johnson, whom we'd met earlier at Estero Llano. Her eyes were moist, but she wasn't the one sobbing.

The crying came from the woman she held in her arms, and as a third woman moved away after giving them both a hug, I realized I knew who was doing the crying.

It was Pearl.

As I looked again at Rosalie, then back once more at Pearl, I also realized something else.

"I think I know who Pearl's grandmother is," I said to my wife.

I walked over to where the two women stood in a weepy embrace. On the way there, I grabbed a tissue from the box on the receptionist's counter and offered it to Pearl.

"Rosalie," I said, turning to the older woman. "I'm so sorry for your loss. I think we just made your granddaughter's acquaintance in the bird viewing area."

Pearl wiped her eyes, sniffled, and looked up at me. "You know my grandmother?"

"We met this morning," I explained. "Rosalie here welcomed us to Estero Llano. I was one of the birders who spotted Mr. Johnson, unfortunately."

At the mention of the dead man's name, Pearl's eyes began to brim with tears again.

Rosalie pulled her in for another tight hug. "It's all right, Perlita," she murmured to her granddaughter. "Everything will be all right."

"If there is anything I can do, please let me know," I said.

Of course, I had no idea what I could possibly do for these two, since we'd just met, and I knew next to nothing about either one of them, except that they were both birders, and Rosalie hated picking produce and Pearl wanted to be an electrical engineer. Somehow, those little pieces of knowledge were not coming together in a momentous way to let me know what I could actually do for either of them. Let's be honest here—my offer was one of those automatic responses you make in times of extreme awkwardness. You never expect anyone to come back at you with a reply.

But Rosalie did.

She told me what I could do.

"You can find out why your friend killed my Birdy," she softly said over her granddaughter's head. Then, her voice like steel, she added, "and I will take it from there."

Chapter Six

She said, 'my' Birdy?"

Luce and I were on our way to the Alamo Inn in Alamo, which was only a short drive from the Valley Nature Center in Weslaco. After Rosalie's unexpected suggestion for my assistance, I'd left the women, taken Luce by the arm, escorted her out to our car, and shared my brief conversation with the grieving naturalist.

"Yes," I said. "I remember that the chief said something this morning about Rosalie and the deceased being close, but I guess I hadn't really considered how close they might be. Now I'm thinking *very* close."

* * *

I pulled into a parking spot along the curb near the side door of an imposing historic white brick building. The door was a deep red, and off to its side hung a sign that read Alamo Inn Bed & Breakfast.

"This must be it," I said, looking up through the windshield at the two-story building. With its straight lines and no-nonsense architecture, the Inn looked like a bank or land office on the set of an Old West movie. When I'd searched for the address on my phone, a brief description had come up noting that the Alamo Inn was housed in the original 1919 building of the Alamo Land and Sugar Company.

"I suppose the owners of the inn have the place furnished with antiques," I said to Luce, checking out the potted plants and antique bench beside the red door. "Eddie told me this place books up years ahead of time. He said he was lucky they had a suite available for him on such short notice."

Luce laid her hand on my right arm and waited for me to look at her.

"Bobby, you don't really think Eddie is involved in this, do you?" Concern had filled her voice, along with a note of fondness for my old friend.

"Of course not," I assured her, then on second thought, amended my answer.

"I mean," I said, "I don't think Eddie killed Birdy, but the fact that his bottle of Aquavit was found beside a dead man does make me think he's somehow involved. Not like he's responsible for what happened," I clarified in response to the alarm in my wife's eyes. "But somehow, Eddie's tripped into something he probably shouldn't have."

Luce removed her hand and nodded. "You think we can help him?"

"I think we have to," I replied. "Hell may have no fury like a woman scorned, but a woman bent on vengeance can't be far behind. I know I wouldn't want to find myself in Rosalie's bad graces. She sounded scary. If Eddie wants to make it back home to Minnesota after he finishes this consulting job with the border patrol, he'd better come up fast with proof that he's completely innocent of Birdy Johnson's murder, or he'll have a certain petite naturalist hunting him down."

On that note, we climbed out of my SUV, and I tried the doorknob of the red door. It was locked.

"Bob! Over here!" Eddie called.

I turned around to see Eddie walking in our direction from across the street.

"I'm in the garden suites," he said, hitching a thumb over his shoulder. "Come on over and meet the boys."

Luce and I crossed the street and the parking lot that lay between the historic inn and its newer annex. Composed of two two-story buildings facing each other, the architecture reminded me of college dorms with outdoor hallways: a series of doors fronted with open walkways, and between the two buildings a lush garden of flowering roses, rosemary, red salvia, lantana, and a collection of other native shrubs and trees. As we got closer, we could hear laughter floating out from several open doors, along with some acoustic guitar music. I noticed Eddie had an open beer bottle in his hand, and his flannel shirttail hung loose out of his pants.

"What's this?" I asked him. "A birders' dormitory? You got a party going on?"

"Nah," Eddie said. "Birding's done for the day, and so everybody kicks back a little. After our morning, we all figured we could use some winding down."

He gestured with his bottle towards the second floor balcony where a fellow sat on a lawnchair, strumming a guitar in the late afternoon sunshine.

"You met Schooner this morning," my old friend said. "He spends two months here every winter. Says it's better than a Club Med vacation."

"Yo, Minnesota!" Schooner greeted us from the second floor. He picked out the first few chords of an old rock-and-roll tune I thought I recognized from hearing it on my dad's stereo turntable when I was a kid. "Smoke on the Water!" he called, lifting his hand to brush back some of his white mane. "You joining us for dinner before we go work on the parade float?"

"I want to take them to see the vultures first," Eddie called back to Schooner.

A Northern Mockingbird swept past us on its way to land in the branches of a tree in the garden between the buildings. I followed its flight and spotted an Inca Dove perched on one of the tree's lower branches, not far from where the Mockingbird landed.

"You can get a bunch of species right here at the Inn," Eddie said. He'd obviously noticed that my attention had followed the Mockingbird. "According to Keith—he's the owner here—they've had a bird count of 166 species in the two blocks around the Inn."

He pointed at the blooms in the garden. "You see the flowers in there? Every time I walk by, hummingbirds are in there nectaring."

"Last year, I saw a zone-tailed hawk fly right over the parking lot," Schooner called to us. "Hey, have you seen the parrots yet?"

Two more men came out on the second floor balcony from open doors. The short one with the tropical shirt I immediately recognized as Paddy Mac, and the fellow with the bandana still wrapped around his head was, of course, Gunnar. I vaguely wondered if they always traveled in a flock.

"Do members of the MOB get a discount here?" I called up to the men. "Or is this the only place in the Lower Rio Grande Valley where they'll rent rooms to birders wearing Hawaiian shirts?"

The men laughed and toasted us with their own open beer bottles.

"Come on," Eddie said. "I want to show you something."

He led Luce and me to his own door and opened it to reveal his first-floor suite, which was more like a little apartment with its full kitchen, living room, bedroom, and bath.

"Looks comfortable," I told him. "How long have you been working on this consulting gig?"

Eddie shut the door behind him and walked over to the small dining table covered with electronic equipment.

"Only about a week," he replied.

I followed him over to the table while Luce went to use his bathroom.

"What is this stuff, Eddie? Rosalie told us you're working with the Border Patrol on sensors."

Eddie nodded. "Well, she's partly right. I'm working with the Border Patrol, yes. But we're past simple sensors these days, Bob. I'm testing a new radar recognition program they're using with the drones they've got deployed along the American-Mexican border."

"Drones?"

"You betcha. More fences and more boots on the ground can't do what a drone can," he explained. "Drones give us eyes in remote spots, Bob. We've got mountain ranges along the borders that no patrol can adequately cover, making it prime terrain for hiding illegal immigrants. But with the drones, we get the surveillance data, dispatch troopers to intercept the movement we've picked up, and bingo! We shut down the traffic."

"There are that many illegal immigrants coming into the country that we need a drone fleet?" I asked.

"It's not just people crossing the border that we're looking for," Eddie clarified. "We're looking for any kind of illegal activity, and that includes drug shipments. In a three-month period a year or so ago, the drone surveillance led to fifty-two arrests, and the recovery of more than 15,000 pounds of incoming marijuana."

"Holy smokes," I said.

"Don't know how holy those smokes were, but I do know they were illegal." Eddie picked up some kind of keyboard and tapped out a sequence on the keys. "Birdy Johnson asked me to check out the recognition system in hopes I can refine it to distinguish between adults and children. The radar can already differentiate between humans and animals, but if we could determine that children are involved, then we could get protective services involved faster and get those kids the help they're going to need sooner."

I studied the equipment on Eddie's table a moment longer before I registered his mention of Birdy Johnson.

"Birdy Johnson was the old friend who asked you to take the job?"

Eddie nodded.

I blew out a lungful of air. "Rosalie thinks you killed Birdy."

"Of course, she does," he responded. "She heard me arguing with him about the drone's design the other night while we were sorting grapefruit for the MOB float for the Citrus Parade. I told him it was trash, and he didn't take my criticism kindly, so he said I was a dumb Norwegian. I probably would have punched him in the face if I'd been a foot taller, but since I'm not, I stomped on his foot."

"You picked a fight with Birdy Johnson?" Luce asked.

I turned to find her behind me, her face even paler than her normal Minnesota winter white.

"Are you okay?" I asked her. "You don't look so good."

"I don't feel so good," she said. "Too much sun, I guess."

"You want to lie down?" Eddie suggested.

To my surprise, Luce agreed. My wife can usually put the Energizer Bunny to shame when it comes to endurance; the fact that she did an immediate about-face and headed back towards Eddie's bedroom told me her sudden ill feeling was more than too much sun.

I hoped she wasn't coming down with a cold. Getting sick could put a real crimp in our plans for the rest of our winter break here.

"She'll be fine," Eddie said, obviously reading the look of concern on my face as I watched my wife leave the room. "She wouldn't be the first Minnesotan to be felled by the hot chile peppers down here."

"We didn't have any chiles today," I told him. "We had barbeque at Fat Daddy's. Good barbeque, and plenty of it."

I returned to our conversation before Luce had made her entrance and quick exit.

"So," I summarized, "Chief Pacheco not only has your bottle of Aquavit, which was found near Birdy's body, but he also has eyewitnesses to a fight you had with him?"

"Shoot!" Eddie said, sounding annoyed. "I bet that's where I lost my Aquavit. At the MOB's garage. I was passing it around to everyone there before I insulted Birdy."

"Wait a minute," I said. Eddie was telling me too much at once for me to keep it all straight. "You insulted Birdy? I thought you said you were trash-talking the drone."

Eddie walked over to his little kitchen and opened the refrigerator door. He pulled out an unopened bottle of beer and offered it to me, but I shook my head.

"Suit yourself," he said and uncapped it. "Birdy designed the drone, Bob. He's an avionics engineer from way back. He used to work at NASA."

The framed wall photo of Birdy and Buzz at Fat Daddy's popped into my head, and I began to connect some dots.

"That must be why Birdy was involved with the SpaceX program, then," I said. "He used to work in the space program when it was all government-owned. Now that it's spawned private industry looking to establish a profitable business, the companies probably love getting experienced ex-NASA folks on board to help develop the whole idea of commercial space tourism."

I described the framed photo to Eddie, and another connection occurred to me. "Do you know if Birdy was at NASA while Buzz was an astronaut?"

Eddie nodded again. "That's where they met," he said. "But I don't think Buzz was an astronaut, or at least, he never made it into space as one. If I'm remembering this right, Buzz Davis was kicked out of the astronaut program just before he was scheduled for his first flight. He had a drinking problem."

"But Luce said she recognized him from a parade in St. Paul when she was a kid," I recalled. "She said he was an astronaut."

"He was. He trained as an astronaut decades ago," Eddie conceded. "Those guys were the cream of the crop back then. Heroes in the making. But even so, a few of them never made it into space, because of medical disqualification at the last minute or because a space launch was scuttled. If Buzz Davis was in a parade back then, the organizers must have decided not to hold his disqualification against him."

I thought about the man I'd met that morning on the park deck. He could have been the poster boy for healthy retirement with his tanned skin, clear eyes and athletic stride.

"He must have gone through rehab and changed his evil ways," I said to Eddie. "Buzz Davis glows with healthy living."

"And he wouldn't take a sip of my liquor the other night, either, now that I think about it. Unlike Paddy Mac and Schooner." Eddie shook his head. "Those boys could be world-class professionals when it comes to boozing, let me tell you."

I picked up a few pieces of equipment from the table and turned them over in my hands while I digested Eddie's observations about Buzz Davis and my new-found colleagues of the MOB. "So how are we going to get you off the chief's list of suspects, Eddie?"

"Find out who did kill Birdy Johnson," he replied. "But let's have some dinner first. I'm starved. And then I'm taking you and Luce to watch the biggest flock of ugly buzzards you've ever seen."

Oh, good. If anything could instantly restore my wife's spirits, it would be a flock of birds.

Although, I had to admit, vultures might be a stretch, even for Luce.

Chapter Seven

As it turned out, Luce opted out of going to dinner in favor of taking a nap at Eddie's and heating up a can of minestrone she found in his kitchen cupboard. She insisted she'd be fine, and Eddie and I should go enjoy tamales and burritos at the Tex-Mex restaurant around the corner from the Inn. By the time we got back, she had color in her cheeks again and felt a lot better, so all three of us hopped into my car and headed for the Frontera Audubon Society to see the nightly vulture show.

A short time later, I pulled into the long driveway off South Texas Boulevard that led to the headquarters of the society. Set on fifteen acres of what used to be a family citrus orchard, the preserve was a surprise to first-time visitors with its native thornscrub, wetlands, and butterfly gardens almost in the middle of the city of Weslaco. Luce and I had walked the thicket trail at the preserve on our second morning in the Valley and seen a score of different warblers, along with several hummingbirds and a couple of Black-bellied Whistling-Ducks. Now, as we parked the car in front of the closed wrought-iron gates, I spied a White-tipped Dove perched in one of the trees on the other side, with two Inca Doves nearby.

"You sure we can park here?" Luce asked Eddie.

"No problem," he said. "The gardens and visitor center close at 4:00 p.m., but there are generally a few cars here to watch for the vultures coming to roost for the night. Although I think the stink of all the droppings from the birds discourages some birders from coming to see it."

Eddie waved a hand in the direction of the grove of tall dead trees silhouetted against the sky in the growing dusk.

"Perfect habitat for Turkey Vultures," he said. "Not so great for all the houses around it, though. I can't imagine that hundreds of noisy smelly vultures roosting near your home is good for resale value."

I looked up and a Turkey Vulture glided over me, only about twenty feet off the ground. With another beat of its wings, it sailed toward the dead trees. In a wide circle around the vultures' roost, house lights were beginning to come on. As Eddie had noted, the scavengers' gathering place was practically in the middle of a city residential area.

As more vultures sailed in and the dark flock grew to include hundreds of the birds, the noise level increased until the air seemed filled with the cries of the vultures, and the trees were shrouded in black forms.

It would have made a great scene for a slasher movie.

"Creepy," Luce observed, echoing my own evaluation. "Definitely creepy."

The sound of shots punctured the vultures' chorus and I instinctively ducked behind the car, pulling Luce down with me.

"Are those gunshots?" she asked, total disbelief in her voice. "We're in the city, for crying out loud."

"This is Texas," I reminded her. "Guns are household appliances."

More shots rang out. A flurry of black wings flew out of one of the dead trees.

"Somebody's shooting at the vultures," Eddie called above the din.

I smacked my forehead with my hand. "That's right," I said. "When we visited here yesterday morning, the director told us some of the residents in the area hate the vultures so much, they occasionally shoot BB guns at them."

Luce stood up. "It's still being irresponsible, firing BB guns in a neighborhood. Someone could get hurt."

Another barrage of shots sounded. Luce ducked back down beside the driver's door of the car where I was still crouched.

"I got news for you," she said. "We're not in Kansas, anymore, Dorothy, and those last rounds were not BBs, either."

Great. Just what I didn't want to hear. I was taking cover by my car while a bunch of gun-happy lunatics were waging a turf war with a flock of vultures.

"Eddie?" I called out. "You okay?"

There was a moment of silence, and then a string of curses erupted from the other side of the car.

I bolted, hunched over, around the front of the car and found Eddie sitting near the front tire, his hands wrapped around his right calf. A dark stream ran down his jeans.

"Some idiot shot me," he said, still swearing. "Do I look like a vulture to you?"

Chapter Eight

Chief Pacheco stood in the headlights of his cruiser watching the paramedics from the ambulance tending to Eddie's gunshot wound in the back of their van. Luckily, Eddie had only sustained a bullet graze across his upper calf and the emergency personnel were able to clean and wrap it sufficiently. Nevertheless, I'd already told him Luce and I would be taking him straight to the local emergency room for a thorough exam as soon as the paramedics finished with him.

"That gunshot wasn't meant for a vulture," Pacheco said when I joined him in the glare of his headlights. "The vultures are up in the trees, not down by a car door."

I glanced at Eddie and the medics in the back of the open van. Luce stood off to the side of the van, talking with another police officer.

"Yup, I kind of figured that out," I said.

The chief crossed his arms over his chest and looked towards the vultures' roost. I waited for him to say something else about Eddie being a target, but the silence lingered.

And lingered.

Since I highly doubted Pacheco had developed a sudden interest in observing the habits of roosting buzzards, I guessed something else was occupying the man's thoughts. And since he was standing only a few feet away from where Eddie had landed in a shooter's sights, I also guessed the chief was mulling over the coincidence of two violent acts in one day that involved two men who knew each other.

I knew that's what I was mulling over.

Okay, maybe not "mulling," exactly.

More like *Holy crap! someone was just shooting at Eddie, and this morning, a friend of Eddie's, got his head cracked and a canoe turned over on top of him.*

Needless to say, this was not how I envisioned my third day of birding in the Valley to turn out.

"Who knew you three were coming out here to see the vultures tonight?" Chief Pacheco finally asked, his gaze still on the dead trees of the vultures' roost.

The question hit me in the gut like a sucker punch. For a moment or two, I couldn't speak. When air returned to my lungs, my voice came out with a squeak.

"You think whoever shot Eddie . . . you think we talked with him?" I tried to force my words into coherent sentences. "We know the shooter? Are you kidding me?"

Pacheco turned his head towards me and despite the dark of the falling night, his eyes were sharp and glowing. They reminded me of the eyes of the Barred Owl that I'd spotted one evening in early November from my bedroom window. It was already dark outside, and I'd walked into our bedroom, which was upstairs, to pull the curtains before turning on the room's overhead light, but just as I reached for the curtain cord, I glanced through the window and froze. On the other side of the glass, maybe ten feet away at my own eye level, sat a full-grown Barred Owl. His implacable dark eyes latched onto mine, and I felt an almost palpable chill run down my spine.

This must be how a rodent feels just before it suddenly becomes dinner, I thought.

Then, in the blink of an eye, the owl flew away, its big broad wings gliding into the darkness.

I blinked my own eyes then at the memory, and focused on Pacheco's question.

Who knew that Eddie, Luce and I were going to be here tonight?

"Birders," I said. "The birders staying at the Alamo Inn. Schooner, Gunnar and Paddy Mac."

"They tell anyone else?"

I shrugged. "I have no idea. Why would they?"

I felt Luce's hand slip into mine. "What are you talking about?"

I repeated the chief's question for her.

"I think we may have said something to the naturalist here at Frontera when we visited yesterday morning," she said. "She was the one who first told us about the vultures' roost and some of the trouble they've caused. I think we told her we would try to see them tonight."

"Cynnie Scott," Pacheco said. "She's a local legend when it comes to birding. She's probably the most outspoken bird conservationist along the Lower Rio Grande Valley. She's also the president of McAllen's seniors' birding club." He glanced away for a minute in Eddie's direction. "They like to call themselves the MOB," he added.

"We know," I said. "We were recruited today to help them with the float for the parade. We were going to head over there after seeing the vultures, but now we're taking Eddie to the hospital instead."

The chief lapsed into silence again, his gaze back on the vultures in the trees. He wasn't exactly given to idle chitchat, I decided.

Luce squeezed my hand. "Eddie's about ready to go, by the way."

"I'll take Eddie to the hospital," Pacheco informed us, returning his attention to our conversation. "You go work on the parade float. And do me a favor—talk about this shooting tonight. See what kind of reactions you get from the other people there."

He paused and pinned his sharp eyes on me again. "I'd be curious to know."

I held his gaze for a moment or two, measuring the man's intensity.

"Curious" was putting it mildly. I had the feeling he would have liked to strap a hidden microphone on me and listen in on every word I heard for the next few hours. Someone—or somebodies—in the MOB must have been added to his suspect list since Eddie had been grazed by a bullet. And since I was the new kid in town, who better to send into a crowd of suspects than an innocent bystander just passing through?

Great. So now I was not only going to be a member of the MOB, but I was going to be a snitch, too.

"Are you serious?" Luce asked Pacheco. I had no doubt she had come to the same conclusion I had: the chief was hoping I'd do a little undercover work for him. "You want my husband to gather information for a police investigation for you?"

"Only if he wants to," Pacheco replied. "I said it was a favor, not a requirement."

I looked from the chief to my wife and thought about Eddie crouching behind my car and getting shot. This time around, it was me giving her hand a squeeze. "If I can find out anything to help Eddie, I'm going to do it, Luce. You know that."

She nodded in the dim light coming from the surrounding vehicles and gave me a wink.

"Your reputation as a sleuth must have preceded you," she said.

"Or my reputation as an idiot," I replied. "Either way, let's do this."

I offered my hand to Pacheco for a handshake to seal the deal. "I'm on your team, Chief. Me and the doll," I added in my best B-grade movie gangster voice, "we're going after the MOB. We've got a score to settle and a grapefruit to nail."

Pacheco shook my hand uncertainly.

"Does he always joke like this?" he asked Luce.

"Oh, no," she told him. "Only when he's involved in murder investigations."

The chief gave me another dark look, and I knew exactly what he was going to say. *You've been involved in other murder investigations?* I bumped my wife's shoulder to thank her for opening that particular can of worms.

"You've been involved in other murders?" Pacheco asked a moment later.

Okay, so I was off by one word.

"A few," I admitted. "Maybe . . . five. Or six. I've sort of lost count now."

"It's an occupational hazard for him," Luce explained. "He's a birder who happens to find bodies."

Pacheco looked from Luce to me. "Not that I'm trying to discourage you from birding here, but the next time you're thinking about heading south from Minnesota?" His face was deadly serious. "Consider Florida instead."

Chapter Nine

Wow," I said. "That is probably the ugliest parade float I have ever seen."

Luce and I were standing just outside the open doors of the well-lit three-car garage in a well-to-do neighborhood in the city of Mission, where the MOB's float was being constructed. From what I could see, the float consisted of a flatbed truck with a bunch of chicken wire fencing sticking up near the truck cab. In front of the fencing were mounds of yellow grapefruit and a clotheshanger draped with what looked like a terminally emaciated six-foot tall Great Kiskadee with a broken neck and only one eye.

"Bob!" Luce hissed at me. "Someone will hear you!"

"That's sort of the idea," I whispered back. "Better they hear it now when they can still do something about it, rather than when the float starts down the street in the parade and everybody runs away screaming. That kiskadee looks like a refugee from a teen slasher movie."

Any further comments I wanted to make on the float's lack of aesthetic appeal were cut short by Schooner's welcoming greeting called out to us via a loudspeaker mounted on the top of the truck cab.

"Yo, Minnesota!" his voice boomed from the garage. "Let's show these Texans how to build a float!"

That remark earned him a chorus of outraged voices from inside the garage, asserting that real Texans needed no one's help, that nobody does anything better than a Texan can, and that, if the rest of the country followed Texas's lead, we'd all be a lot better off.

I held up my hands in surrender. "We're just the hired help," I assured the crowd of older birders that converged on us in front of the garage. I nodded at Paddy Mac and Gunnar the Bandana Man, and let my eyes rove over the other faces, thinking one or two looked familiar from the deck at Estero Llano that morning. "If we haven't met yet, I'm Bob White. Hi, kids."

A flurry of handshakes and quick introductions followed as each of the MOBsters said hello to us before returning to their construction tasks on the float.

"I said the same thing about that kiskadee costume," a short and round older lady said to me, patting my arm in a motherly way.

It took a moment or two, but then I recognized her as the straw-hat lady from our morning disaster. I'd had no idea that her hat had been hiding a too-red hair dye job, but I sure couldn't miss it now.

It was almost fluorescent.

"I'm Poppy Mac," she introduced herself, "and I heard what you said. You'd think with all the money this club has in its pockets, we could spring for something fresh. But you know these old men, they'll be darned if they'll spend two nickels for something new if they can jimmy-rig it out of something old."

She smoothed a strand of red hair behind her ear.

"Tightwads," she confided in me. "Bunch of old tightwads. Take my husband, for example. He won't buy new batteries for his hearing aid because he says that it works most of the time. MOST of the time isn't good enough, but he won't replace them until he's stone deaf."

Paddy Mac came up beside her and wrapped his arm around his wife's shoulder. If he'd heard her criticism of his financial habits, he didn't show any sign of it, or maybe Poppy was correct.

He hadn't heard a word because his batteries were on the fritz again.

"Ah, I see you've met my darlin'," he said, giving his wife a loud smacking kiss on her wrinkled cheek. "If she had her way, we'd only be slicing up top grade citrus to use on our float instead of the bruised leftovers. Not that anyone can tell the difference when you've got ten thousand orange halves covering the sides of a truck, mind you, but for my Poppy, it's first class all the way or not at all."

"Oh, get to work," Poppy said, pushing Paddy back towards the garage. "I'm not seeing any sides of a truck covered with chicken wire, let alone citrus, yet."

"Don't be rushing us, darlin'. Haste makes waste," he reminded her. "We don't need any accidents in building this float."

Paddy turned to me and winked. "I spent some time in insurance, and you wouldn't believe the money that gets poured into accident settlements, including parade claims."

He toasted me with the beer can in his right hand. "Safety first, Minnesota."

A giggling Poppy pushed him back to work on the float.

"Bob, you remember Cynnie Scott, don't you?"

Luce was beside me, gesturing towards the woman with whom she'd been chatting. "We met her yesterday morning at Frontera Audubon."

I nodded to Cynnie. "Of course," I said. "But at the time, I had no idea you were involved with this motley crew. I also didn't know you were a local birding legend," I added.

Cynnie, a striking woman with a heavy braid of silver hair swinging down her back, laughed. "That's a polite way of saying I've been around a long time. Which I have. Which also means I should know better than to get roped into the annual frenzy of building a float for the Citrus Parade, but here I am."

She glanced around to see if any of the other MOBsters were nearby, then leaned into me and said, "Luce told me you saw the vultures tonight at Frontera, and that there was a shooting. I hope your friend will be all right."

Before I could say anything, Cynnie shook her head. "I can't believe it, but at the same time, I can't say I'm completely surprised. Tensions have been running awfully high here in the Valley the last few months since the politicos approved the SpaceX installation. Conservation activists are furious, while the economic development people are drooling in anticipation. People are taking sides: conservation or SpaceX."

She leaned in again and dropped her voice lower.

"Between you and me," she confided, "I've been expecting somebody to start taking pot-shots at the vultures, figuring no one would complain if he killed them, since our legislature seems bent on selling out our natural resources to big business. It only takes one step in that direction to set off a stampede."

Cynnie's disgust with her lawmakers was clear, and her words reminded me of what the chief had said about the locally revered birder—that she was the most outspoken bird advocate in the area. In a place like the Lower Rio Grande Valley where birding tourism generated big bucks for the community, I assumed that made Cynnie Scott the darling of all the merchants and businesses who shared in that profitable industry. On the flip side of that community coin, she may have been a thorn in the side of groups that championed causes contrary to her own. Whether it was the preservation of a vulture roost or rerouting a road to conserve breeding areas, the staunch bird lovers I'd met over the years weren't afraid to take their concerns into public arenas.

To be even more blunt about it, Cynnie Scott may have made serious enemies among local community leaders with her advocacy of birding and birds. It wouldn't be the first, and certainly not the last, time a birder didn't flinch at ruffling the feathers of powerful people.

"Where exactly is this SpaceX base going to be built?" Luce asked her. "From what you're saying, it sounds like it's more than another economic development that will be impinging on natural habitat. Which is bad enough," she quickly added, "but I think that, these days, all birders know of at least a few projects in their own areas threatening habitat."

Luce was voicing my thoughts as well. Birds and economic development were always at odds, it seemed to me. Of course, that made perfect sense since they both wanted use of the same pieces of land (or air space), but for radically different reasons. Developers wanted to use natural resources for human purposes. Birds needed those resources for their survival.

Some people think that activism on the behalf of protecting bird species began in the 1990s with the very public battle over preserving habitat for the Northern Spotted Owl in the face of logging operations in the Northwest of the United States. But the truth is that a concern for birds' survival surfaced in the last years of the nineteenth century, when the extinction of the Passenger Pigeon and the alarming decline in the population of Whooping Cranes led to a reappraisal of human impact on wildlife populations. In 1900, America's first conservation legislation was signed into law by President William McKinley. Known as the Lacey Act, it charged the Secretary of the Interior with the responsibility to safeguard game and wild bird populations from commercial exploitation. Over the years, other wildlife conservation legislation was enacted, including the Endangered Species Preservation Act in 1966. Finally, in 1973, President Nixon signed the Endangered Species Act, which continues in force to this day.

That doesn't mean our national mandate to protect endangered species isn't challenged, or circumvented, by special interest groups.

Two years ago, a wind turbine project along the shores of Lake Erie sparked national headlines with the confrontation it caused between energy companies and the American Bird Conservancy over bird deaths that resulted from birds flying into turbines. In Minnesota, a proposal for a similar wind energy project was defeated by state conservation activists out of concern for safeguarding Bald and Golden Eagles that nested in the area. From what we'd already heard about the SpaceX project since our lunch at Fat Daddy's, it appeared to be the lightning rod of the moment for birding issues around this part of Texas.

Cynnie's expression morphed from disgust to astonishment.

"You don't know where the spaceport's going in?" she asked. "I just assumed you did, even if you are new to the area. This disaster has been brewing for a while."

Luce and I both gave her blank looks.

"We only learned about it earlier today," I explained. "It's like a lot of commercial developments—if it's not directly impacting your part of the country, you don't hear about it."

"Well, this one should be making the national news big-time. It's in Boca Chica Beach," Cynnie said. "East of Brownsville, near the U.S.-Mexican border, five miles south of South Padre Island. It's next to a state park in the Boca Chica subdelta of the Rio Grande."

Okay, I could see why people might be upset about developing a beach. Proximity to beaches was probably jealously guarded in a hot and dusty state like Texas, but in this particular area of the state, you practically bumped into a state park boundary every time you turned around. The airport in Harlingen, in fact, was about a stone's throw from Hugh Ramsey Nature Park, which formed part of the Harlingen Arroyo Colorado, one of the nine World Birding Center sites in the Lower Rio Grande Valley. Heck, you could almost bird in Hugh Ramsey from your plane seat while waiting for take-off.

Cynnie must have read the lack of understanding on my face, because her next comment hit me like a knock-out punch.

"It's on the flyway," she emphasized. "THE flyway that branches into the Mississippi and Central flyways. If they build a space launch complex on that piece of land, you can bet it's going to disrupt the migration patterns of hundreds of thousands of birds. That particular beach area is vital to the health of the migratory corridor into North America. We're talking about over 500 species of birds being impacted."

Holy crap.

Cynnie looked at my stunned face.

"Now, does that sound like a stupid idea or not?" she asked me.

Again, holy crap.

"How did they get past the Endangered Species Act?" Luce asked. "Or the Migratory Bird Treaty Act? They both charge the federal government with conservation responsibilities mandated by law."

Whoa. My wife had obviously recovered from her shock faster than I had from mine if she was referencing federal guidelines.

"That's what we had working for us in Minnesota," Luce continued. "The Treaty Act helped us put the heat on the Vikings football organization to modify the construction of their new stadium. Their original design called for about two football fields' worth of glass, which is really attractive to people, but deadly for all the birds that fly right into the glass because they don't realize it's there. On top of that, the stadium isn't far from where the Mississippi River cuts through downtown Minneapolis, which meant all that glass would be a deadly hazard for birds migrating along the flyway."

Oh yes.

The Vikings.

Their defense of the stadium project had brought new meaning to the word "oblivious." After the initial outcry from bird lovers about the non-friendly bird design went nowhere, the local city councils took up the cause. They passed resolutions calling for bird-safe glass to be used, only to be equally ignored by the Minnesota Sports Facilities Authority, the group established by the state legislature to oversee the construction and operation of the new stadium.

(And did I mention that the stadium was being built with almost a half billion of taxpayer dollars? Too bad we, the taxpayers, can't cough up that kind of money for the purchase of more state nature preserves, but I guess that's a bone that I—and my fellow conservation advocates—will just have to keep gnawing on.)

Anyway, birders' protests got louder, a citizens' group was formed, the media jumped in, the Migratory Bird Treaty Act was invoked, the Minnesota Legal Defense Fund for Migratory Birds was organized, until finally, the sports authority began working with 3M to develop a product to use on the glass to make it bird-safe.

Cynnie nodded. "I followed that fight. We've got the same problem here, basically, but even worse. We've got two flyways in jeopardy, and building glass is the tip of the iceberg. We're looking at a huge building project that'll reconfigure the landscape, deafening spacecraft launches that'll drive away species, and masses of people in what is currently one of the most important birding sites in the western hemisphere. "

"But the environmental guidelines," I protested. "Even the Federal Aviation Administration has to comply. How can SpaceX get the approval to build a commercial spaceport where two major flyways converge?"

"Bureaucracy can be bought," the naturalist observed, "or at least mollified. The deal is that the FAA completed their review, and gave SpaceX the green light if it took measures to mitigate the environmental damage."

"Measures?" Luce echoed. "Mitigate? So it's okay to do some damage, as long as it's not as bad as it could possibly be?"

For a few moments, all three of us were silent.

"Holy crap," I finally said out loud.

"My feelings exactly," Cynnie said. "It's like every other ecological disaster created by man. As long as it's not in your backyard, tough luck for the people who do live nearby. It has to get personal before the big shots will do anything about it."

She smiled grimly. "And that's my job. I aim to make it personal for everyone."

For some reason, her smile didn't leave me all warm and toasty.

"Yo, Minnesota!"

Schooner was standing a few feet away from our glum little group.

"You folks going to nail some grapefruit, or just yak all night?"

"Just bringing them up to speed on our local tragedy-in-the-making," Cynnie said.

Schooner struck a pose, his hands on his hips and his eyes narrowed. "You saying our float is a mess? I'll have you know we spent a week of long nights at Roosevelt's planning this masterpiece of ornithological beauty. And some of those nights we were even sober."

"Roosevelt's is a favorite micro-brewery of the birding community around here," Cynnie informed us. "It's in McAllen, and the owners are good friends of mine. They usually kick in a donation to our Festival Fund, too. Which they should," she added, "since our MOB members make liberal contribution to the profit side of the restaurant's ledger."

"With reason," Schooner insisted. He took Luce's arm and steered her toward the lit garage. "The best sandwiches in town," he told her.

Cynnie and I followed Luce and her escort into the float construction zone. Once inside, the sound of pounding hammers, shooting nail guns, and shouted instructions filled the air. I walked over to the side wall of the garage where three sketches of the MOB float were pinned to a large corkboard.

The first one showed a side view of the flatbed, with a human-sized Great Kiskadee surrounded by poster-sized photos of other birds common to the Lower Rio Grande Valley. In the drawing, the big bird was waving, presumably to the delighted parade crowds.

That explained the scary giant kiskadee currently draped on the float: some lucky individual was going to wear the creepy costume and be a goodwill ambassador for both Great Kiskadees and the McAllen Older Birders. The one-eyed detail was obviously a nod to the notorious one-eyed kiskadee specimen currently frequenting the area—the same one Luce and I had encountered at Estero Llano after running into Crazy Eddie this morning.

The second drawing of the float depicted what would be a ten-foot-by-ten-foot map representing the convergence of the two flyways that had created the area's stellar reputation as a world class birding location. It looked like the map would have a base of chicken wire covered in different types of citrus to create the two migration corridors: the Central flyway was going to be a path of oranges, while the Mississippi flyway would be a river of limes. According to the sketch, Texas was going to be a mosaic of lemons, with the nine World Birding Centers marked by stars composed of ruby red grapefruit.

The third sketch showed the front of the truck cab decked out like the head of a Green Jay. What in the world the float builders were going to use for the brilliant sapphire blue of its head, I had no idea; unless some innovative grower in the Valley was about to unveil a new variety of blue citrus, I assumed there was going to be some heavy spray-painting of oranges going on before the float made its public appearance in the parade. Having already observed firsthand at the Alamo Inn that many of the MOBsters regularly indulged their taste for beer, I made a mental note to myself to be sure I stood clear of any spray painting that might be scheduled for later lest I ended up on the float myself as a real Texas rarity: a blue Bob White.

A round of hoorays came from the other side of the garage, and I turned from my study of the float sketches to see a grim, but politely smiling, Buzz Davis stepping into the garage from the door that led into the attached house.

The man was tough, I decided. Stoic under pressure. His best friend had been killed this morning, and here he was putting in an appearance with a bunch of birders building a float for a parade. Then I guessed that either Buzz owned the house and the attached garage, or he was on very familiar terms with whoever did, and he was here for the companionship of friends in a very difficult time.

"Let's hear it for Buzz!" Schooner's amplified voice thundered in the garage. "Thanks for the use of your high-tech hangar here!"

That answered that question. This was, indeed, Buzz's property.

And a mighty fine property it is, I thought, looking at the dark green Porsche parked in the far stall of the three-car space. If I remembered correctly from seeing the house when we drove up to the garage, the attached home was both expansive and expensive: a solid brick exterior with plenty of wrought iron fixtures, including open balconies on the upper level that overlooked a fountain that tumbled into a wide basin in the center of the brick-paved driveway.

Just because you washed out of the astronaut program didn't mean you couldn't still make a lot of money, I guessed. I wondered briefly what business had brought Buzz Davis his wealth, and when I remembered that Rosalie had said he was a Winter Texan, I realized that meant that Buzz probably had another home someplace else.

I wondered if it was as spectacular as this one.

No wonder Poppy Mac had complained about the decrepit kiskadee costume. If the MOB had this kind of money behind it, they could probably afford to buy any costumes they wanted. Heck, with that kind of money, they could buy all the costumes in the state.

Luce interrupted my case of green envy by loading a crate of yellow lemons into my arms.

"Follow me," she commanded.

As ordered, I trailed my wife to a section of the garage where a large sheet of chicken wire was slowly being transformed into the map of the migration corridors I'd seen in the sketches. I looked from the empty expanse that would become the state of Texas to the crate of lemons I was holding.

"There is no way these lemons are going to cover that whole area," I said. "We'll be lucky if we can get the panhandle out of this crate."

A beeping noise behind me caught my attention and I turned to see Buzz Davis driving a small lift truck toward me.

It was piled high with crates of lemons.

"Let me guess,' I said, stepping aside so Buzz could lower the front lift's cargo onto the garage floor. "Lemons for Texas."

Buzz climbed out of the little truck and patted me on the back. "Welcome to the MOB, Bob. I hope you like the scent of lemons, because you're going to be wearing it for a few days by the time we finish with the float. You know, Birdy—"

His voice faltered, and I saw his jaw tighten and his eyes tear up. He looked up at the garage ceiling and let out a long breath. When he looked at me again, he had a smile on his face.

"Birdy used to say we were making something a lot better than lemonade out of lemons when we built this float every year for the parade." Buzz took another long breath. "He said we were building an invitation to every person at the Citrus Festival to get outside and appreciate birds."

Luce took the crate from my hands and put it on the floor. "I'm so sorry for your loss, Buzz," she told the old man. "I've heard from some of the other birders here that you two had been close friends for almost fifty years."

"That's right," he said. "We flew combat missions together in Vietnam. Got shot down together. Can you believe that's where Birdy got hooked on birding? In the middle of a war zone."

A forced laugh escaped from his mouth, and he shook his head. "Whoever would have thought he'd die from cracking his head open because he tripped over a log birding?"

"Is that what the chief said?" Luce asked.

I immediately took her elbow and steered her toward the other birders.

"Ixnay on the eriffshay," I said out of the corner of my mouth. To Buzz, I waved goodbye and said we'd check back with him later.

"Why would the chief tell him that?" Luce asked me when I'd walked her around the chicken wire map to pick up a nail gun sitting on a bench. "He told us Birdy's death is being handled as a homicide."

I handed her the nail gun and picked up a box of nails to go with it.

"Luce, think about it. Birdy was at the park with Buzz. Buzz was the last one to see him alive, apparently. Chief Pacheco has to consider Buzz a suspect for that reason alone."

I saw a trio of birders kneeling on the map, working on arranging the limes to form the Mississippi flyway. I saw that Gunnar was among them, his signature bandana now tied into a sweat band around his head.

"Where should we start with the lemons?" I called to him.

"Take your pick," he called back. "Anywhere inside that yellow painted outline is fine. That's a whole lot of Texas to cover."

I grabbed a big tray of lemons that had already been halved.

"I figure that the chief told Buzz it was an accident to keep the real details of the investigation under wraps, so whoever killed Birdy won't know the police are already looking for him," I continued, laying out my theory to Luce. "If Buzz is the murderer, you don't want to tip him off that you're onto him."

"But the Aquavit," Luce protested. "It was Eddie's bottle."

"Which he said he lost here, working on the float," I noted. "Any of these people could have picked it up . . ."

Luce finished my thought. "And then coincidentally happened to drop it near where Birdy's body was found?"

Our eyes met over the tray of lemon halves.

"You know," I slowly speculated, "if you were planning to kill someone, and you found a personal item that would link its owner to the murder scene, maybe you'd think that'd be a good idea—plant false evidence to point to someone else as the killer."

"Like a bottle of Aquavit," Luce said. "But that means anyone who was here with Eddie . . ." She let her sentence trail off.

I nodded. Almost in unison, we both turned our heads to scan the faces of the people in the garage.

Buzz, Schooner, Gunnar, and Paddy Mac had all been at the park this morning when I'd spotted Birdy's leg beneath the overturned canoe. Schooner and Paddy Mac had, in fact, been part of the small clutch of birders with us when I noticed the Green Kingfisher at Alligator Lake, just before I caught a glimpse of Birdy. Another person in the garage had also been at the scene, I now realized. Poppy Mac, Paddy Mac's wife, was one of the women with us at Alligator Lake.

As for the rest of the birders working on the float, I couldn't recall if any had been at the park, but there was no rule I knew of that said a murderer had to hang around until his victim was found. For that matter, there was no reason at all to think the murderer had been on the park deck with us as Chief Pacheco began collecting statements. I knew I sure wouldn't stay around if I'd killed someone—I'd make a beeline for the border.

Huh.

In this case, the border was right there—the Mexican-American border, that is.

For just a second, I had a flashback to Buzz and Rosalie on the park deck before Luce and I set off to Alligator Lake and found a dead man. Buzz had made some comment about immigrants not being welcome and Rosalie's response gave me the feeling she was offended.

"That's right!" I said, then realized I'd said it out loud, which was why Luce was giving me a funny look.

"Rosalie's an immigrant," I said, laying the tray of lemons back on the bench.

"What are you talking about?" my wife asked.

"I thought you could read my mind," I told her. "You always seem to know what I'm thinking. Here." I took her hands and placed one on each side of my head. "Can you hear me thinking?"

"I think the sunscreen we bought yesterday isn't working and now your brain has fried along with your arms," Luce suggested.

She removed her hands. "No, I can't hear you thinking. What are you talking about?"

"This morning, at the park when we met Rosalie and Buzz. She was upset when Buzz made the crack about immigrants not being welcome in Texas," I explained. "Pearl told us Rosalie grew up, poor, in Mexico, and that she really appreciated the opportunities she found in America. I bet she sympathizes with the illegal immigrants who risk so much to find a better life in the United States, and she was offended by Buzz's attempt at a joke."

Luce studied my face a moment, then tapped me on the chest with the end of the nail gun. "And what does that have to do with anything?"

I opened my mouth, but nothing came out.

"I'm not sure," I admitted. "But there's something about the border being so close to where Birdy was killed. I'm sure of it. I just don't have it all figured out yet."

Luce pointed her nail gun at the tray of lemons. "How about we work on getting this map done? Maybe by the time we finish Texas, you'll have another clue."

I picked up the tray of lemons again and followed her to the edge of the yellow outline where she dropped to her knees to start attaching the fruit halves I handed her.

I didn't want another clue.

I wanted to solve the case and keep Crazy Eddie from getting killed.

Because in my experience, once a birder sets his sights on a particular bird, he doesn't give up until he gets it. I didn't want to find out the same was true of whoever had set his gun sights on my old friend, instead of the vultures, at Frontera Audubon.

Chapter Ten

After an hour of marinating in lemon juice as we worked on the panhandle of Texas, we were recruited by Gunnar to help him finish the lime ribbon that represented the Mississippi flyway. Since it was getting late (and nailing slippery lemons was taking longer than I had expected), the three of us decided it made more sense to combine our efforts to totally complete one section of the map and leave the rest of Texas for the next night.

"I heard you guys talking about Eddie getting shot at over at Frontera," Gunnar remarked after instructing us where to nail the last crate of limes. "That's scary stuff. I knew your friend was working on some hush-hush deal with the Border Patrol, but he must have really ticked off somebody if he's dodging bullets."

I set the crate down beside Luce and sat on the floor beside her where she was preparing to nail the halved fruits onto the chicken wire map. We exchanged a quick glance and a slight shake of the head to tell each other that neither of us had mentioned to anyone in the garage that the shooting was being considered as anything other than the work of a disgruntled and aim-challenged vulture hater.

Yet Gunnar had assumed Eddie was the target, not the buzzards.

"Why do you say that?" I asked him, trying to sound casual and not like I was snooping for Chief Pacheco, which, of course, I was. So far, everyone I'd told about Eddie's "accident" had responded with the same assessment as Cynnie Scott—that the anti-vulture roost crew had some gun-happy vigilantes in their ranks. Gunnar was the sole birder to suspect something more was going on.

"That's what Paddy Mac said when he told me about it," Gunnar replied, then looked up from the limes he was slicing in half. "That's not what happened? Did Eddie get shot or not?"

I debated how to answer that, but before I could say anything, Gunnar chuckled.

"I should have known. That Paddy's always pulling my leg. Always looking for a whopper of a story to tell. Last week he tried to convince me he was in the witness protection program. He's got that Irish blarney streak in him for sure."

Gunnar shook his head and took another lime from the pile near his cutting board.

"He was doing the same thing this morning," he said, setting the lime on the board. "He came up with a dozen detailed scenarios for how and why Birdy died. Personally, I thought the one most probable was where Birdy stumbled into a drug deal gone bad."

He grabbed another two limes and lined them up with the one already set on the board. With one stroke of the sharp butcher knife in his hand, he sliced neatly through all three. His technique reminded me of Luce when she was doing her chef thing in our kitchen at home; calculated, extremely efficient, and very, very skilled.

"I actually saw a drug bust on the street in Alamo one night when I was out owling," Gunnar continued as he methodically sliced more limes. "You couldn't miss it, really. A truck squealed to a stop, with a cop car behind it, and two more patrol cars zoomed in from the opposite direction. Three guys piled out of the truck cab, guns blazing. The police took the shooters down, cuffed them and stuffed them into the back seats of the squad cars."

"Whoa," I commented.

Gunnar looked up and smiled, his wispy white eyebrows lifted almost to where his bandana circled his head.

"You don't have that happen where you go owling?" he asked in mock surprise. "Anyway, it wasn't until Chief Pacheco told us to have some respect for Rosalie's grief and to quit with the theories and butt out, that Paddy shut up."

Gunnar cut through another three limes, then added as an afterthought, "I think Paddy forgot that Rosalie is Pacheco's mother. He's real protective of both her and his niece Pearl, I've noticed. I've seen the chief out at the park more than a few times in the last month, talking with Rosalie. Actually," he paused, "not talking so much as arguing."

I almost dropped a handful of lime halves on Luce's arm.

"Wait a minute," I said, needing to hear the family tree again. "Rosalie, the naturalist, who was Birdy's close friend," I said, giving a little pointed emphasis to the word "close," "is Chief Pacheco's mother?"

Gunnar blinked. "Yes. I'm guessing from that look on your face you didn't know that. Am I right?"

"You're absolutely right," I said, still trying to keep everyone's relationship to everyone else straight. "But Pearl—her last name is Garcia, I think."

"That's right," Gunnar said. "Her mom, Rosalie's daughter, married a fellow named Garcia. The story is he was in the U.S. illegally and had to go back to Mexico, and Pearl's mom went with him, leaving Pearl with her mom Rosalie. You can ask Rosalie about it. She'll be happy to tell you what she thinks of immigration laws that break up families."

Ouch.

As a high school counselor in Minnesota, I heard a lot of similar opinions from the families of our immigrant students. Whether they were Latino, Somali, Hmong or Russian, every one of my culturally diverse students related tales of splintered families, long separations and ethnic discrimination. Coming to America was as much an ordeal for some of them as it was a promise for a better life, and my students' experiences were all on the legal side of the page.

I couldn't imagine what a mess it was for families that tried to enter the country illegally—the kinds of families that Eddie's surveillance drone was designed to find and help.

Eddie's drone.

Eddie had come to Texas as a favor to Birdy.

Birdy was involved with Rosalie.

Rosalie disliked the immigration laws.

"And Birdy told me we would have to keep an eye on Eddie, for everyone's sake," Rosalie had said.

And now Birdy was dead, and Eddie was getting framed for his murder.

By Rosalie? Had her relationship with Birdy gone south—way south—when he became involved in creating more effective border control with drones, because of her own family's heartbreak? As I recalled from our initial encounter this morning, Rosalie hadn't taken kindly to Buzz's inference about unwelcome migrants. And while she'd been suitably bereft with shock and grief early in the day, she'd impressed me as a tough cookie when she accused Eddie of Birdy's murder when she'd shown up at the Valley Nature Center.

How bitter was she about her family's situation? Bitter enough to kill Birdy and pin it on Eddie? If that were the case, she could basically take out two birds with one stone: the border patrol's drone designer and the drone's test engineer.

"Bobby?"

I realized Luce was waving her hand back and forth in front of my eyes.

"I think you've seen one lime too many tonight," she said as I pulled my attention back into the garage. "We're done with the Mississippi flyway, and everyone is calling it quits for the night."

I glanced around the garage and saw only a few people left near the float's truck cab, which, to my surprise, was actually beginning to bear a resemblance to a Green Jay. I looked for the kiskadee costume on the flatbed, but it was gone. Our chicken wire map, however, was a beautiful field of various citrus fruits, except for an empty patch in the middle of the state that we could easily finish off tomorrow night.

I stood up and then helped my wife to her feet. She swayed for a second, and I mentally kicked myself for letting us labor so long on the float when Luce had been feeling under the weather earlier in the evening.

"Are you all right?" I asked her.

She gave me a sheepish grin. "I think I got up too fast, and all the blood rushed out of head. Plus, I forgot I didn't have any dinner. I guess sneaking sections of oranges doesn't quite cut it as high octane fuel for creating parade floats."

Nonetheless, I kept an arm around my wife's waist as we walked out of the garage.

Which turned out to be a good thing, since I had to swing her out of the way as a car came roaring down the driveway, swerving dangerously close to where we were walking.

"Hey!" I shouted at the driver, though I couldn't see his face since I was almost blinded by the car's headlights.

The car squealed to a stop in front of the open garage bay and the driver's door flung open. Out tumbled a young man, who quickly caught himself from falling flat on his face after he caught one foot in the car door frame. He pulled himself back up by grabbing onto the side of the door and hoisting his body erect to lean against the side of the car.

"No wonder he didn't see us," Luce observed. "The idiot is wearing dark glasses. At night."

"Actually, I doubt he'd see any better without them," I replied. "That kid's drunk."

"Oh, my," Luce whispered, her voice barely a breath.

Startled by her sudden change in tone, I searched my wife's face.

"Are you sure you're all right?" I pressed her.

But she wasn't looking at me. Luce's eyes were riveted to the car in front of the garage.

"It's a vintage Mustang, Bobby."

I glanced back at the car.

Luce was right. The drunk driver had a classic Mustang.

Though I'd never been interested in cars other than to have them transport me to birding spots, my wife had grown up with a father who adored classic sports cars and shared that love with his only child. Looking at Luce, you'd never guess she was a grease monkey at heart, but believe me, the woman knew her way around a V-8 engine. In the years I'd known her, in fact, plenty of our weekend birding trips had ended with a classic car show in some remote community.

I've learned that birders weren't the only people who loved a good road trip.

The car's noisy appearance had likewise attracted the attention of the last folks in the garage, but before anyone could say anything, the inebriated driver yelled out.

"Uncle Buzz!" the young man shouted, his long arms splayed across the roof of the car. "You need any more lemons tonight?"

He held up one hand to reveal a lemon in his palm.

"I got it at the bar," the kid's voice slurred. "I told the bartender I knew just who could squeeze the juice out of it. You're good at that, aren't you, Uncle Buzz?"

From our spot on the driveway, I saw Buzz Davis walk out of his big garage and head towards the boy and the expensive car.

In the sudden quiet of the night, the older man's words carried to where I stood.

"I want you out of this car and inside the house," Buzz told the young man. "Now."

The kid stood his ground, still leaning against the car roof.

"Or what?" he challenged his uncle. "Are you gonna ground me permanently, like good old Birdy grounded you? You hated him for that, didn't you? I get that, now. Payback is a wonderful thing, isn't it, Uncle Buzz?"

"You don't know what you're talking about, son," Buzz said, his voice tight, as he got closer to the kid. I could practically feel the older man's muscles tensing.

"I'm not your son!" the young man shouted at him. "I hate your guts! Everyone around here worships the ground you walk on, except for me, because I know what a two-faced liar you are!"

"Holy buckets," Luce breathed beside me. "The kid is not only drunk, but begging for a fight."

"And he's not leaving until he gets it," I said, watching the young man ball his fists on the top of the car while he glared at Buzz.

The kid wasn't about to move, let alone go quietly into the house.

Whether that was because he was physically unable to stand unaided thanks to his alcohol level, or because he deliberately wanted to antagonize his uncle, I couldn't be sure. Either way, I could see where this confrontation was going.

It was headed south, and not in a good "escape from winter" heading-south sort of way.

Unless I missed my guess, Buzz Davis was about two seconds from grabbing his nephew and forcefully removing him to the house.

And I was fairly certain that, if he didn't land the first punch, his nephew would.

Crap.

I was going to have to break up a fight between a senior citizen and a twenty-something kid.

And I figured the odds were with the old guy winning.

I started toward the two men, but then I got a last-second reprieve.

"Yo, Mustang Mark!" Schooner shouted, running out of the garage to round the opposite end of the kid's car from where Buzz was closing in. "Hey, buddy! Over here!"

The kid's head swiveled away from Buzz and toward Schooner. He squinted into the glare from the well-lit garage to see who was calling for him.

"Hey, it's the old hippie!" he grinned at the birder, his angry exchange with his uncle apparently forgotten for the moment. "What are you doing here?"

Schooner threw his arm around the kid's shoulder and led him away from the car and towards the garage. "Finishing the float, man. You and I met right here, last night, remember? We talked cars and microbrews."

I watched Schooner escort the kid into the garage and then up to, and through, the house door, avoiding the other birders, who, like me and Luce, had been accidental witnesses to what had almost amounted to a train wreck between Buzz and his nephew. A car door slammed, and my attention swung back to Buzz, who was now imitating his nephew's stance, his palms spread on the roof of the Mustang, his eyes directed down at the concrete driveway.

A few muted goodbyes were called to Buzz as the final float workers drifted off to the cars parked in the drive beyond the garage's third bay where the green Porsche gleamed in the overhead lights.

A love of sports cars ran in Buzz's family, I surmised, my attention shifting back to the vintage Mustang from the Porsche. Buzz continued to stand, braced at the side of the car, and I recalled what Eddie had said about Buzz's curtailed career as an astronaut: Buzz had been kicked out of the space program because he had a drinking problem.

Buzz had been an alcoholic.

My eyes went to the house door at the back of the garage where Schooner had ushered Buzz's nephew.

Apparently, that was another thing that ran in the family: alcoholism.

"I have to say something to him," I said quietly to Luce.

She nodded and turned away to go to our car, leaving me to speak alone with Buzz.

I was probably five feet away when Buzz broke the silence that had descended on the driveway.

"His name is Mark," the one-time astronaut said, still gazing down at the ground. "He's my sister's grandson, and his mother, my niece, didn't know what to do with him anymore, so I said I'd take responsibility for him. Get him straightened out."

Buzz looked up at me, the planes of his weathered face harsh in the bright glare of the garage's lights.

"I'm not doing a very good job, am I?" he remarked.

"It's not my place to say," I told him. "But I can assure you there are places you can find help."

Buzz attempted a half-hearted smile.

"I know," he said. "Been there, done that. If you haven't heard about it already, I'd be surprised. I'm an alcoholic, Bob. I've been sober for thirty years now, but you don't cure this disease. You live with it . . . if you're lucky and you get treatment. If you're not lucky, it kills you."

He tipped his head towards the house door.

"I don't want to lose Mark, but he's been fighting me tooth and nail. He'd actually been doing a lot better lately. He was beginning to develop a new interest in things. But today . . ." His voice trailed off. "Ever since he heard about Birdy, he's been a mess. I'd almost say a disaster waiting to happen, but obviously, the waiting is over."

Buzz leaned down and retrieved the lemon that his nephew had dropped.

"That was the comment about me squeezing the juice out of the lemon," he explained. "Mark knows he's a mess, the 'lemon' of the family, and he says I'm squeezing all the fun out of him by trying to get him into treatment."

Buzz tossed the lemon in the air and caught it easily. "But I'm trying to save his life . . . the same way Birdy Johnson saved mine."

He leaned his back against the car and held the lemon up in front of his face as if he were studying it.

"The hardest part," he said, avoiding my eyes and keeping his own trained on the fruit in his hand, "was that Birdy had to ruin my career in order to do it."

Chapter Eleven

The faint alarm of warning bells began to ring in my head.

Here it comes, the bells told me. *Buzz Davis is going to tell you his life's story.*

Crap. After all my years of experience working with high school students, you'd think I'd get used to people unloading their tales of woe on me, but the truth was, I'd be unspeakably happy if I never again had to listen to another soul-baring monologue from a person who was basically a stranger. At work, I got paid to listen, but for some reason, it seemed that even when I wasn't at work, people wanted to confide in me. I didn't know why that was. Maybe it was the open posture and kind smile I honed during my graduate school training to become a counselor.

Or maybe people just thought I was a sap, and I'd listen to anyone.

Whatever the reason, I decided it wasn't going to happen tonight. I was on vacation, and it was late, and I'd started the day by finding a dead man, stood steps away from my old friend when he was grazed by a bullet, and spent the last few hours getting lemon and lime juice squirted in my eyes.

I mean, really, how much could one man take?

"Buzz," I said, "it's late. Go to bed. Get some sleep. It's been a terrible day."

And I walked away to get in my car with my wife.

"What did he say?" Luce asked me as I pulled out of Buzz's driveway and pointed the car in the direction of the Birds Nest, a cozy bed-and-breakfast retreat we'd booked for the week that was actually a private guest suite on the property of another birder.

"He's a recovered alcoholic and Birdy Johnson ruined his career," I told her, giving her the condensed version of our conversation.

"He said that?" Luce sounded shocked. "Are you telling me Buzz Davis just admitted to you he had a motive to murder Birdy Johnson?"

I glanced at her face, which was softly lit by the streetlights we passed as I drove out of Mission and crossed the city limits into the residential neighborhoods of McAllen.

"Yes, I guess I am telling you that," I answered, though I hadn't even thought of it in those terms till she mentioned it. All I'd considered was that I wanted to call it a night and get some sleep.

"Shouldn't you call Chief Pacheco or something?" Luce asked. Her voice sounded more animated than it had been all evening. "Don't you think he'd want you to share that information with him as soon as you got it?"

"I'll share it tomorrow," I told her. "Besides, I know you haven't felt real good since this morning. I thought you'd just as soon turn in for the night."

"I got a second wind."

"I didn't," I told her. "I'm beat. And you know what? I'll bet that Chief Pacheco is already looking into Buzz and Birdy's history, which means he probably knows about Buzz getting kicked out of the astronaut program because of the booze. And if his mom, Rosalie, was as close to Birdy like it seems she was, the chief probably also knows about any bad blood between the two men."

Or, I mentally added, *if there was some kind of trouble between Rosalie and Birdy because of his drone work for the border patrol.*

I realized I had another suspect to add to my list of birders who'd been at the park when I spotted the dead man: Rosalie Pacheco.

Pacheco as in mother of Chief Pacheco.

Geez. Could the list of suspects get any more tangled in relationships?

Another possibility hit me.

Could the chief himself be a suspect?

The young National Guardsman we'd met at Fat Daddy's—Pacheco's third or fourth or whatever cousin—he'd mentioned that the chief had stayed in the area to clean up the border zone. At the time, I hadn't thought much about what that meant exactly, but now I had to wonder. Was "cleaning up" about drug smuggling or illegal immigration? If his mother Rosalie was bitter about immigration laws because of her granddaughter's family situation, maybe the chief had his own ax to grind on his niece's behalf.

But that didn't tell me which camp the chief was in.

Pacheco may have sympathized with the illegal immigrants because his own family had been split apart as a result of immigration law.

Or, because his own family had been split apart by immigration law, the chief might be determined not to let that same thing happen to anyone else's family.

Which still didn't tell me if Chief Pacheco might have had a motive to kill Birdy Johnson.

And then something else popped into my head.

The Guardsmen had ribbed Guardsman Pacheco about his girlfriend, Pearlita, the Citrus Queen of this year's festival.

Rosalie's granddaughter—the chief's niece—was named Pearl.

Pearl Pacheco was the Citrus Queen and Guardsman Pacheco's girlfriend.

"Luce," I said, pulling up to the security gate that guarded the driveway to the Birds Nest. I leaned out of my window and punched the access code into the console. "I just realized that Pearl, Rosalie's granddaughter, is the Citrus Queen."

The wrought iron gate slid back, and I drove past our host's home to the attached guest quarters where we'd spent the last few nights.

"And her boyfriend is the young man we met at lunch," Luce confirmed. "I know. I heard a couple of the birders working on the float tonight talking about the Citrus Queen and her court. All the birders know Pearl because of her work at the Valley Nature Center. I guess you missed out on that conversation."

Yeah, I guess I did. Luce must have picked up those tidbits of information while I looked over the float sketches tacked up on the garage wall. Maybe I should ask my wife to start wearing a wire so I could overhear all of her conversations.

That wasn't too creepy of an idea, was it?

Clearly, I was more tired than I thought.

We got out of the car and collected our birding gear from the back seats to take inside with us. From the other side of the guest quarters, I heard the call of an Eastern Screech Owl. Our birding host, Rhonda Gomez, had a veritable birding oasis in the middle of McAllen. Enclosed by a brick fence, her one-acre yard regularly attracted local and migrating birds, and Rhonda's own backyard bird list had more than thirty species on it.

The fact that we could see so many birds right outside the suite was one of the main reasons we'd chosen to stay with Rhonda. If for some reason, all we could force ourselves to do once we got to the sunshine and warmth of the area was to lie around on chaise loungers and soak up heat, we could still come home with some Texas specialties on our lists, like Great Kiskadees, Green Parakeets, and Chachalacas.

As it had turned out, both Luce and I had a lot more energy for birding once we arrived in McAllen, so we had yet to lay around on a lounger. When you find yourself in a birder's paradise like the Lower Rio Grande Valley, it's a crying shame to not spend every waking moment exploring one of the hundreds of excellent birding spots in the area.

"Rhonda left us a note," Luce said, picking up a piece of stationery from the little bistro table where we had breakfast every morning outside our bedroom. She read through it and handed it to me.

Hey, Bob. Just wanted to let you know that I had a visit this afternoon from a Chief Pacheco asking me to verify when you arrived here at the Birds Nest

earlier in the week and what time you left this morning. He said it was part of an investigation, and since I saw the news at noon about Birdy Johnson, I'm guessing you were at Estero Llano when the body was found. Does this mean you're going to be staying in the Valley longer than you had originally planned?
Rhonda :-)

"I don't know if this is good or bad news," I told Luce after reading Rhonda's note. "Good in that we have a witness who can verify our location at the time of the murder, or bad in that the chief felt the need to double-check our statements."

I looked again at the note from our hostess.

"She added a smiley face at the end," I pointed out to Luce. "I guess that means she'd be happy to have us stay longer in the Birds Nest if we have to stick around in the Valley because of the investigation."

"As long as our staying longer in the Valley doesn't mean arrest and a stay in jail," Luce amended. "That would definitely not be my idea of a fun way to end our winter getaway."

"Our getaway, huh? You've been spending too much time around the MOB, doll-face," I said. "You're beginning to talk like they do."

"Doll-face?" Luce grimaced. "Where did that come from?"

I opened the door to our room and stood aside to let her go in ahead of me.

"Too many late nights watching old gangster movies when I was in college," I replied. "Either that, or I was a mobster in a former life."

"That would be quite a jump," Luce noted, "from gun-toting hitman to the mild-mannered, sensitive, peace-loving birder I know and love."

She dropped her birding backpack on the big cushioned chair in the corner of the room and sat down on the end of the quilt-covered bed.

"Seriously," she said, "we're not going to have to extend this trip to help clear Eddie of murder, are we? I know you're concerned about him. So am I, especially after someone took a shot at him tonight. But all my instincts are telling me we can't help him, Bobby. We don't know the territory. We don't know any of these people. How can we help?"

I put my Birds Nest key and my binoculars on the dresser next to the bed. Luce was right: we might as well have been chickens with our heads cut off, running in circles, for all we knew about the circumstances surrounding Birdy Johnson's death. Not only that, but by accompanying Eddie to observe the vultures roosting, we'd unintentionally put ourselves near a line of fire. Watching my wife pull off her hiking boots, I resolved this was one crime I was going to leave to the authorities, and this was one birding trip that was not going to go bad.

Except that I was pretty sure we'd already hit the "bad" threshold.

I needed to rephrase that.

This was one trip that was not going to get even worse.

"Tell you what," I said to Luce. "I'll call the chief in the morning, give him the play-by-play from tonight at Buzz's garage, check in with Eddie to make sure he's all right and has the name of a good lawyer, and then we're going back to being birders on vacation. No more sleuthing. Just good birding."

Luce gave me a tired smile. "Right now, I'll settle for a good night's sleep."

* * *

Within thirty minutes, my wife was well on her way to dreamland, the soft sound of her breathing slow and relaxed beside me in the bed.

I, of course, was wide awake, despite my resolution to leave the day's deadly events in the hands of the local chief. As I mulled over the people we'd met, I tried to imagine each one committing murder. Buzz and the chief certainly had the strength to deliver a killing blow to the head, but why would they bother to hide the body under a canoe? And if hiding the body was their intent, why didn't they check to be sure no body parts were still showing? It was, after all, Birdy's foot sticking out from beneath the canoe that had revealed his location.

Which told me that whoever flipped that canoe didn't take the time for a thorough check for total concealment.

Which also told me the murderer was aware of the presence of others in the area who might suddenly appear as they birded.

The murderer was, therefore, familiar with the park and its patrons, so whoever killed Birdy Johnson was no stranger to Estero Llano.

Or to Birdy, because he'd let his killer get close enough to hit him in the head.

I rolled over in the bed, realizing I had no idea what kind of blow Birdy had taken.

But the fact that it was a fatal blow to his head forced me to eliminate Rosalie Pacheco, Birdy's close friend, as a suspect. Rosalie was short, and while Birdy would certainly let her get close enough to hit him, she would've had to swing upward in order to reach Birdy's head. Picturing the petite Rosalie in my mind, I was certain she couldn't muster enough power to kill Birdy with one blow, at that angle.

Buzz and Chief Pacheco, on the other hand, would have found it easy. One of the first things I'd noticed about the chief was his muscular arms, and Buzz, too, looked lean and strong. Either of the men could have fatally injured Birdy, and while it was common knowledge that Buzz had accompanied Birdy when they'd first arrived at the park, no one could be expected to know the chief's whereabouts before his arrival after the 911 call.

Pacheco could have been sitting right outside the park . . . because he'd just left it after killing Birdy.

Of course, that didn't explain Eddie's bottle of Aquavit near Birdy's body, which just seemed much too obvious as a piece of evidence pointing towards my old friend. If Eddie had lost the bottle during a float-building session as he said, then Buzz would be the logical finder of the bottle, and the planter of the same as evidence.

Motive? Birdy had destroyed Buzz's bid for a place in space exploration history when he ratted out his friend's drinking problem. Though Buzz seemed to have done just fine financially, I supposed that could have been an awfully tough pill to swallow when it happened, especially for someone who had worked hard for that opportunity. Losing it not only meant public disgrace and forfeiting a career, but the denial of a personal dream.

And no more parades as an astronaut.

Even worse, it gave your drunk great-nephew ammunition for publicly humiliating you.

Although I didn't think Buzz was so much humiliated by his young relative's verbal attack as he was just completely frustrated with the kid's self-destructive behavior. Besides, as far as I could tell, Buzz's disease was no secret among the MOB. Everyone already knew about it.

Which also meant that Buzz's history with Birdy could be a very convenient motive for a MOBster to use for framing Buzz for his friend's murder. I ran down the list of birders in my head one more time.

Schooner.

Gunnar.

Paddy Mac.

Poppy Mac.

Who among them would want Birdy Johnson to fly away permanently? And who was framing whom? Was one of those four trying to frame Eddie or Buzz? Or was Buzz the murderer and trying to frame Eddie?

And that meant I was back where I started when I first heard Luce's even breathing next to me—wondering who, among the cast of characters I'd met, had killed Birdy Johnson.

Chapter Twelve

Two hours later, I woke up with a start.

No, I didn't have the name of the killer delivered to me in a dream.

A dog was growling.

Very loudly.

Just outside our bedroom.

And then the growling was gone, replaced by crazy loud barking that was moving away across the yard.

I hopped out of bed and ran over to the window next to our door and peered out through the glass.

On the far side of Rhonda's expansive yard, Maddie, her resident English Labrador, was furiously barking at the six-foot-tall brick wall that enclosed the property. The big brown dog was practically dancing with excitement, rearing up to put her paws on the wall, then backing away, and all the while swiping her tail back and forth with what looked like dog-style gleeful abandon. I noticed that the lights in Rhonda's living room flicked on, and a moment later, she was out on the stone patio calling for Maddie.

I opened the bedroom door and called across the large patio that separated our suite from the main house.

"Rhonda, is everything all right?"

In the dim light coming from the living room windows, I could see that Maddie had returned to her mistress, although the dog was still clearly excited about her midnight adventure. Rhonda grabbed Maddie's collar and waved to me.

"We're all good, Bob," she replied. "Some critter must have come into the yard and set her off. I'm so sorry she disturbed you."

"No problem," I called back. "Nice to know we've got a good watchdog looking out for us."

I turned back towards the room and saw a piece of paper taped to our bedroom door.

I pulled it off and held it up in front of me to catch some moonlight to read it.

Go home, Minnesota, or you're going to get hurt, I read.

Call me crazy, but I was fairly certain Maddie hadn't left the note. Last I'd looked, dogs didn't have fingers to write with, and in the absence of either dog paw prints or dog slobber running the ink, I could only assume we'd had an uninvited visitor in the yard.

One that could write.

Talk about topping off a bad day.

I walked back into the room and shut the door behind me.

"What are you doing?" came my wife's sleepy voice from under a mound of blankets.

"Just catching a little fresh air," I told her. "Go back to sleep, honey."

I checked the digital clock on the nightstand. It was two in the morning.

Ah. My mistake. The threatening note wasn't topping off a bad day, after all.

It was just starting a whole new one.

"Bobby," my wife said, her voice more awake. I looked at Luce, who had pulled the blankets down to speak to me. "Next time, you might want to put on some clothes when you go out for air. Just sayin'."

I looked down at my bare feet . . . bare knees . . . bare . . .

"Good idea," I said. "I'll try to keep it in mind."

As I got back in the bed, I really hoped Rhonda was near-sighted.

Or had a really, really short memory.

* * *

Six hours later, I was ready to give the new day another shot. This time, it wasn't a menacing growl outside our door that woke me but the light sighing of wind chimes on the other side of the house. I took a quick shower and surrendered the bathroom to my wife, pulled on some clothes (yes, I can be taught!) and walked out to explore the yard.

A quick scan of the treetops yielded a flycatcher taking a moment's rest from feeding. I listened for a moment, hoping the bird would vocalize, since both the Couch's Kingbird and the Tropical Kingbird were residents in this southern edge of Texas and virtually identical in plumage. The Couch's Kingbird has a much smaller range, though, and is rarely found south of Mexico, while the Tropical branch of the family spans almost the full length and width of South America. The bird I was watching let out a cry just as it took to the air again, confirming with its nasal *pik-pik-pik-pitweer* that it was, indeed, a Couch's Kingbird, giving me a new bird to add to my life list.

Nice score for right outside my door, I reflected, as I also watched a Black-Crested Titmouse flitting among the branches of a bougainvillea bush near the corner of our suite. From the top of one of the large mesquite trees in the middle of the yard came the cackling of grackles. Two birds hopped from branch to branch, and I was able to get a good look at their long, broad tails; these along with their low-pitched buzzing call mixed in with their cackles confirmed they were Great-tailed Grackles.

A panting sound behind me had me turning to greet Maddie as she bounded from the patio to join me in my exploring. Her brown coat glistened in the morning sunlight. As soon as she reached me, she leaned her solid body against my leg and lifted her nose to snuffle at my hand.

"So," I said to the dog, scratching behind her velvety ears, "who did you chase away from my door last night?"

She wagged her tail enthusiastically and leaned even more heavily into my leg.

"Don't tell me you didn't get a name," I scolded her. "I need a name."

To my surprise, Maddie ran for the portion of the brick wall where I'd seen her jumping in the night and buried her nose in the grass near a thorned tree laden with golf-ball-size Key limes. A moment later, she was back at my side, with a shred of cloth between her teeth. She dropped the scrap at my feet and sat, her eyes looking adoringly into mine.

A clue?

I picked up the shred of material and examined it. I could have sworn its faded colors looked familiar.

Like a tropical print.

"Good morning, Bob!"

Rhonda waved to me from the patio. Maddie took off towards her mistress, leaving me alone in the middle of the back yard.

Did the shred of cloth come from last night's intruder, or was it a scrap dropped by birds as they collected trimmings for nests?

I looked up at the dead tree trunk near the corner of the yard that Rhonda had pointed out to me on our first morning at the Birds Nest. She said she referred to the tree as the Bird Condo, since it was filled with holes drilled by birds for nests. According to Rhonda, the tree had housed a family of Black-bellied Whistling-Ducks last spring, and I'd seen pictures of trios of Eastern Screech-Owls perching on another tree limb on Rhonda's acre of suburban bird sanctuary. Knowing many birds scouted far and wide for nest-building materials, it wasn't a stretch of my imagination to think the slip of fabric in my fingers could have come from almost anywhere in the neighborhood, or that it had been lying on the ground for weeks.

At the same time, the shred's location close to where Maddie had barked so vigorously last night seemed too coincidental to completely disregard, so I tucked the bit of fabric into my jeans pocket to hand over to Chief Pacheco in case he wanted to see it.

Now all I had to do was decide what to do about a threatening note taped on my guest suite door in the middle of the night.

Go home, Minnesota, or you're going to get hurt.

Not exactly a whole lot of options there: go home, or get hurt. Why couldn't I have had a few more choices like "Open Door Number Three" or "Pass Go and Collect $200"?

Of course, the more interesting matter to consider was why I had received the note in the first place. Call me suspicious, but I had the uncomfortable feeling my activities of the day before had unwittingly tangled me and Luce into a murder plot that wasn't finished. The fact that my wife and I had now landed on someone's anonymous threat list didn't fill me with a warm and fuzzy feeling, either.

It sort of made me angry.

No. That wasn't right.

No "sort of" about it.

I was angry.

As in *really* angry.

Who did our secret letter writer think he—or she—was? Luce and I had as much right to be here in the Lower Rio Grande Valley as anyone else on the planet. We'd come for a warm vacation and a birding extravaganza, which was the same reason a lot of people headed to south Texas in January. And even if we had blundered into a murder scene as after-the-fact witnesses . . . well, so had a small flock of MOB members. Unless all those folks likewise received a special invitation during the night to get out of Texas, that meant we'd been singled out for a reason.

My angry train of thought came to a screeching halt.

There were only two reasons I could think of for telling a murder witness to leave town: to stay safe to testify later, or to make any possibility of testimony disappear.

It all depended on who did the telling—the law or the killer.

I was pretty sure Chief Pacheco wouldn't resort to taping a message on my door for my protection, nor could I imagine him creeping across Rhonda's lawn to leave me a threatening message. If the chief wanted to get rid of me for any reason, I was confident he had more effective ways to do that; a restraining order could probably do that trick just as easily as coming up with some false reason for arrest.

If, on the other hand, the killer wanted me out of the way, I could only conclude it was because I knew something that could help finger him as Birdy's murderer.

Great.

What did I know that I didn't know I knew, but that the killer did know I knew?

I started walking back to the patio where Luce had joined Rhonda. Both of the women were smiling while they talked, but before I reached them, our hostess vanished into her home, the valiant watchdog Maddie at her heels.

"Rhonda said she was glad to see you were dressed this morning," Luce said, trying to suppress a smile. "For the weather," she added a beat too late. "It's supposed to be a little on the cool side for January along the Rio Grande."

I felt a tiny roll of heat slide onto my cheeks and narrowed my eyes at my wife.

"She didn't . . . last night . . . this morning," I stammered, my cheeks feeling hotter by the moment.

Luce gave me a big kiss smack on my lips and stopped trying to hide her grin.

"No, she didn't," Luce assured me. "Rhonda said she was practically night-blind. She only knew it was you at our door because you called out to her first. She wanted to apologize again for the disturbance."

"It wasn't her fault," I told Luce, handing her the folded note that I'd slipped into my back pocket when I'd gotten dressed after my shower. I watched her face as she read the line of warning.

I tapped the note in her hand.

"This is whose fault it is," I said. "And we're not leaving Texas until we know who wrote it . . . and why."

Luce's beautiful blue eyes turned ice cold.

"Lead the way, Bobby. I think Rhonda was wrong about today's forecast. I have a feeling it's going to get plenty hot after all."

Chapter Thirteen

Chief Pacheco, his assistant informed me when I phoned, couldn't meet with us before ten in the morning, so Luce and I decided to make a stop at Quinta Mazatlan, another of the World Birding Centers right there in McAllen. I'd heard a few of the birders the night before talking about the Curved-bill Thrasher they'd seen there earlier in the week, and I hoped we could repeat their find.

Ten minutes later, I parked the car in the big lot in front of Quinta Mazatlan's regal entrance driveway that was lined on both sides with lush formal gardens. At the top of the drive stood a white adobe mansion that would have been right at home in a sprawling Hollywood mini-series. According to the brochure we picked up at the entrance desk, the mansion was built in 1935 in the Spanish Revival Style and remained a private luxury estate until the city of McAllen bought it in 1998. Eight years later, the historic property was repurposed as a "mansion with a mission," and it was now operated by the city's Parks and Recreation Department as an urban sanctuary dedicated to connecting people with nature through its programs about birds, plants, and environmental stewardship.

Not to mention that the property also offered excellent birding with its native plants and twenty acres of tamaulipan thornforest, which is the ecological biome of that part of Texas and northeastern Mexico.

In birding terms, it meant birds I'd never see in Minnesota.

Luckily, a small band of birders was just about to set out on a morning birding walk around the Quinta Mazatlan grounds with one of the staff guides, so Luce and I trotted out of the impressive tiled entryway to join the group outside on one of the garden paths that opened onto the palm-lined driveway. We said hello to the other three people and then turned to greet our volunteer guide as he came out of the building behind us.

It was the kid from last night.

The drunk driver of the Mustang.

Buzz Davis's great-nephew.

I glanced at his name tag as soon as he got close enough for me to read it.

Mark.

Yup, that was the boy.

Mustang Mark, Schooner had called him.

Although, in the bright light of morning, Mustang Mark didn't look so much like an underage drinker, but more of a much younger version of his uncle Buzz.

A young Buzz with a blond ponytail and somewhat blood-shot eyes.

He introduced himself to our little group, and it was clear from the lack of recognition in his eyes when he looked my way that Mark had no idea we'd almost crossed paths the night before, let alone become casualties of his impaired driving.

"Welcome to Quinta Mazatlan," he said, his voice surprisingly steady and strong. "If you've never birded here before, you're in for a treat. We've documented over 160 species right here on the property, and today I think we're going to see some vireos and warblers, along with our usual suspects of Green Jay, Great Kiskadee, and several varieties of hummingbirds. Situated on the convergence of the Mississippi and Central flyways, we've got one of the best spots on the planet for birding right here in McAllen, Texas."

I couldn't help myself. I nudged Luce with my elbow in her side and whispered, "Imagine that—this is where the Mississippi and Central flyways converge—you learn something new every day, don't you?"

She gave me a small grin and pushed my elbow away.

Mark proceeded to ask each of us in the group where we were from and whether we were new visitors to the area. Of the five of us, two—a man and a woman—were older residents of McAllen who had recently taken up birding as a hobby. Another woman, who was probably in her mid-twenties, was on vacation from Boston on her first birding trip to south Texas. When Luce and I mentioned we were from Minnesota, I thought I detected just a twitch of heightened interest on Mark's part, but he immediately moved on to begin our bird walk by directing us onto the Thornforest Trail.

"This is one of my favorite trails here at Quinta Mazatlan," Mark told us, walking backward to face us, his voice hushed as we followed the trail away from the main driveway. "We have thirty native species of trees . . ."

He stopped mid-sentence and tilted his head in a listening pose.

I heard the call then, too, and looked over Mark's left shoulder towards a cluster of tall scrappy bushes. A fast flitting noise accompanied a tiny yellow-gray bird with two white wing bars as it darted from branch to branch.

"Look at those spectacles," Mark whispered to us, his own neck moving back and forth as he tracked the bird hopping from limb to limb. "It's a White-eyed Vireo. They're generally hard to find, let alone being able to get a good look at, since they move so fast."

All six of us peered into the shrubbery as the tiny bird continued to forage for insects.

"This is the vireo's wintering grounds," Mark informed us. "Both the male and female sing, and if we're lucky, maybe we'll hear them. The birds are fairly secretive, so generally birders hear them more often than see them."

He turned around and led us along the pathway that wound through the forest, stopping occasionally to point out Golden-fronted Woodpeckers, Yellow-bellied Sapsuckers, Inca Doves, and White-winged Doves perched in trees. At one spot on our walk, a small flock of house sparrows were making so much noise in the bushes lining the path that I had to raise my voice to ask our guide a question about the property.

"With all the native plants and trees here," I commented, "I'm guessing you must teach some landscaping for wildlife classes here at the Center. Do you get a lot of people interested in that?"

Mustang Mark nodded enthusiastically. "It's part of our mission. We call it our 'Backyard Habitat Steward' program, and its goal is to help people restore their backyards into natural habitat. We have so many beautiful birds and butterflies in this region that it's fairly simple to attract them into your own yard with native plants. Visitors come from all over the world to see our wildlife, but people who live here can enjoy it every day if they know what to put in their own yards."

"That's true everywhere," I told him. "If you plant the native trees and flowers, you'll get the wildlife that goes with it. All it takes is a little education about natural environments."

"Over there," Luce said, touching my arm to catch my attention. "An Orange-crowned Warbler, about fifteen feet up in that tree."

I followed her pointing finger and caught sight of the warbler. As I looked, a Rufous Hummingbird flew by right in front of me.

"Good eye," Mark complimented Luce as we moved on. "You know your birds. You said you were from Minnesota, right?"

I wondered if he was beginning to connect us with the MOBsters working on last night's float in Buzz's garage. I recalled that Schooner had distracted the boy with his enthusiastic greeting, thereby interrupting the mounting tension between Buzz and his nephew. Taking charge of the inebriated boy, Schooner had pulled him into the house and away from his uncle, at which point I could almost hear a collective sigh of relief from the assembled float workers. I knew I was appreciative of Schooner's fast thinking because it had meant I hadn't had to step up to the plate and resort to my own crisis management experience of breaking up fights.

Granted, most of my experience was with fights that took place in high school hallways or cafeterias, but I figured the basic elements were the same.

Although, Lord knows, there would have been plenty of limes and lemons in Buzz's garage for ammunition.

"We're just in town for the week," I heard Luce tell Mark. "We're trying to visit all the World Birding Centers, but I don't know if we'll be able to fit them all in. There's just too much to see."

"Did you get out to Estero Llano Grande State Park yet?" the young woman from Boston asked. "It's amazing."

Mark agreed. "It's got the largest wetlands of any of the Centers. And I've found some excellent trails in the woodlands that a lot of people miss. It's almost like you've got the whole place to yourself . . . and the birds. Very secluded. I highly recommend it."

Interesting.

Mark knew the trails of Estero Llano.

I wondered if he'd learned them from his uncle, since Rosalie had indicated that Buzz and Birdy were well-known birders at the park. Last night, I hadn't even considered that Mark might be into birding, but this morning, I'd learned otherwise—Mustang Mark was extremely knowledgeable and skilled as a birder. To my surprise, he was also very likeable; he laughed easily with our little group of birders and engaged everyone in conversation.

All in all, Mark seemed like a pretty good guy. He reminded me a lot, in fact, of his uncle Buzz, who also seemed like a pretty good guy.

Unfortunately, also like his uncle, Mark had a disease he needed to address. For everyone's sake, I hoped that happened sooner, rather than later.

"I heard somebody found a dead man out there yesterday," the older fellow in our group volunteered as we returned to the main drive of the estate. "One of our Winter Texans. I think he had a heart attack."

"That's right," his companion said. "He was DOA at the hospital."

For a split-second, I thought *oh my gosh, another body out there? Does the park have a quota system or something?*

But then I realized the two birders were referring to my own discovery of Birdy Johnson's body, and that, like Buzz and the other MOB members last night, no one was privy to the details of the death the chief had shared with Eddie, Luce, and me. I stole a quick glance at Mustang Mark and was surprised by his reaction to the local man's statement—I could have sworn our guide's tan went green around the edges.

Again, interesting.

Based on Mark's bad boy behavior and insults to his great-uncle last night, I would have assumed the younger man was no admirer of either Birdy Johnson or Buzz Davis, blood relation or not. Yet just now, the colorful addition to his skin tone immediately struck me as a visceral reaction, something Mark had virtually no control over. If he hadn't seemed so focused as our guide, I might have thought he was having a morning-after bout of nausea, but aside from his bloodshot eyes, Mark seemed no worse for his overindulgence the night before.

In fact, unless I missed my guess, the reminder from the birder that Birdy Johnson was dead hit Mark right in the gut, and my counselor instinct told me Mustang Mark was experiencing a physical reaction of intense remorse.

He'd virtually tossed Birdy's death into his uncle's face during his drunken rant.

Pulling a stunt like that would make anyone feel sick . . . once you realized what an insensitive jerk you'd been.

Now, on the sober side of that scene, Mark must have been kicking himself for the way he'd acted, knowing that no amount of apologizing could ever completely undo the hurt he'd caused his uncle. If that were the case—and I hoped it was for Buzz's sake, because it would mean that Mark wasn't a total moron—then maybe the bad boy behavior was just that: bad behavior, and not evidence of a bad boy.

A loud scratchy cry of *kis-ka-dee* called a halt to my rumination as a flash of yellow, black, white, and reddish-brown flew over my head and settled to perch in the upper branches of a tree.

"Great Kiskadee," Mark said, his tan back to its previous shade, his voice smooth and professional. "One of the largest members of the Tyrant Flycatcher family and a Texas specialty. That black mask he wears?"

He pointed at the bird that continued to make its raucous call.

"It works like the black smears athletes apply under their eyes: it reduces glare," he explained. "That gives the kiskadee an edge for hunting insects in bright light or snatching small fish or snails. A great example of natural adaptation."

A light gasp escaped the lips of the Boston birder.

"It's only got one eye," she said.

"Great Kiskadees are aggressive," Mark replied. "They'll attack larger animals, like snakes or raptors, that try to raid their nests. It's inevitable that they might sustain injuries. Protecting what's yours is a key to survival in the natural world, but it doesn't make it any less dangerous. Or deadly."

I found myself staring at Mark as he spoke.

More precisely, I was staring at his shirt.

His Hawaiian shirt.

With a tropical print.

That was clearly ripped along one side.

I realized Mark was watching me stare at him.

"Have we met before?" Mark asked.

Chapter Fourteen

Before I could answer, the older woman in our group grabbed her companion's arm and loudly whispered.

"Look, everyone! Is that a Curve-billed Thrasher over there?" she asked the rest of us.

I hesitated only a moment longer before turning in the direction the woman was pointing. Perched on top of a lamp pole near the front drive to Quinta Mazatlan was a large, grayish-brown bird. Even though I thought I could see the downward cast of its bill, I lifted my binoculars to my eyes to make sure.

"It's the thrasher," I confirmed to our group. "It's got the long thin bill that curves downward, and the eyes are yellow-orange."

"He's also got the faint spots on his chest," Mark said, his own binos to his eyes. "He's been here all week. You folks are getting the royal treatment, today, seeing all these birds."

He lowered his binoculars and checked his wristwatch. "I need to wrap this up with you since I've got a student group coming. Third-graders. Noisier than a flock of Great Kiskadees, let me tell you. Enjoy your day and be sure to take a look around inside the mansion."

With that suggestion, he turned his back on us and strode briskly away.

"What do you think of him?" Luce asked me, tipping her head in the direction Mark had taken back towards Quinta Mazatlan's main entrance. "I never would have imagined him as such a personable tour guide after his performance last night," she added.

I nodded in agreement.

"He's a good kid, I think," I said. "He's definitely a good birder, and he must have had decent references to land a volunteer position here."

"But?" Luce asked. She could recognize the uncertainty in my voice as easily as she had identified the Orange-crowned Warbler during our birding walk.

"But he's got some issues with alcohol and accepting his uncle's help, I think. I got the impression he felt really badly about Birdy's death when that other birder brought it up," I said, "but he covered it well and just went right on with the tour. Who knows? Maybe Birdy's death will make Mark realize life is short, and he needs to get his act cleaned up and make peace with his uncle."

I slipped my fingers in my pocket to make sure the scrap of material Maddie had fetched for me was still there. Part of me wished I had taken it out and held it next to Mark's shirt to see if the print matched, and part of me was convinced I'd moved past suspicious to paranoid.

I hardly knew this kid. I hadn't even spoken with him at Buzz's place, and I was fairly certain he'd been oblivious to my presence on the driveway, seeing as he'd been so focused on railing at his uncle. And yet I thought I'd caught a spark of special attention on Mark's part when we told him we were from Minnesota—a spark, I considered, that may have led to his query about our having previously met.

A query which I was able to avoid answering, by the way.

So what in the world could Mustang Mark possibly hold against me enough to warrant a very early morning foray into a fenced yard to leave a threatening note?

I left the shred of fabric in my pocket and took my wife's hand.

"We've got a little time before we go to meet the chief," I said. "Let's take Mark up on his suggestion and go check out the mansion. I want to see what a 'mansion with a mission' looks like."

Palatial, I'd say.

With its high-beamed ceilings, tiled floors, palm-lined courtyard, Grand Hall and airy light spaces, the mansion was about a zillion degrees nicer than my own place of work, which was a broom-sized cubbyhole in an ancient brick high school. Combined with the extensive outdoor spaces and gardens, the mansion was well-equipped to host a wide variety of events, and judging from their program listing of educational events and activities, the City of McAllen was putting Quinta Mazatlan to good use as a model for native habitat preservation.

I wandered into the gift shop alcove just inside and left of the mansion's main entrance while Luce made a stop at the ladies' room. I was considering buying us a matching pair of sweatshirts emblazoned with the Great Kiskadee and Green Jay when I thought I recognized a woman's voice coming from behind the registration desk and cashier's station across the entry area.

I leaned back to see across the entry, but a visitor was paying for his purchase at the desk and obscured my view of the woman. A moment later, he left the desk, and I recognized Poppy Mac, her red hair flaming, tending the register. Paddy's wife wore a Quinta Mazatlan name tag, though hers was marked with "STAFF," whereas Mark's had been labeled "VOLUNTEER."

"Bob White!" Poppy called as soon as she caught sight of me. "Welcome to Quinta Mazatlan. Did you take a bird walk this morning?"

I walked over to the counter and set the sweatshirts on the glass surface.

"We did," I told her. "And our guide was Mark, Buzz Davis's great-nephew."

"You want these?" Poppy pointed to the shirts.

I nodded and she entered the information on her sales terminal, looking down through the bottom half of the glasses perched on her nose.

"Mark is an excellent birder," she said, tapping in the price. "Really, one of the most talented volunteers we've got. He's just such a loose cannon sometimes. That comes to $65.73. Do you want to use a credit card?"

She glanced up at me, and I handed her my card.

"Well," she continued, "you saw him last night at Buzz's. Such a shame. Disgraceful, really. I was so embarrassed for both of them. I know Mark has a drinking problem, but he shouldn't be taking it out on Buzz. Buzz is only trying to help. And especially last night, what with Birdy's accidental death and all. Buzz and Birdy were so close, and I know that Mark knows that. I can't imagine why he was so awful to Buzz."

She looked quickly around to see if anyone else was in the store, then leaned over the counter to confide in me.

"You know what?" she asked.

I started to say something, but I guess she'd already determined that I knew nothing, because she went right on without any prompting from me.

"I've heard that there are all kinds of secret drop-off places for drug deals in the area," she informed me, "and Mark certainly knows his way around all the parks. Of course, he's young, too. Young people can do such stupid things, can't they? I think Mark's into drugs, if you want to know the truth."

Actually, I didn't.

What I really wanted was to add Texas birds to my life list, enjoy a week of warmth and sunshine with my wife in January, and find out what it was like not to have to help anyone navigate a crisis for a few days. So far, I'd managed two of the three, but that last bit—about crisis—wasn't playing out too well in the last twenty-four hours, and I didn't have high hopes for it to magically go away in the next few hours, either.

But gee, you can't always get what you want, can you?

Especially when somebody decides to bring that crisis right to your front door.

Or, in my case, to my guest suite's front door.

I watched Poppy efficiently fold the sweatshirts and slide them into a Quinta Mazatlan Nature Store bag. Luce joined me at the counter and said hello to Poppy.

"How often do you have a shift working here?" my wife asked her, making polite conversation.

Poppy printed my receipt and slipped it into the bag. She looked at Luce over the top edges of her eyeglasses.

"I just started a month ago," she told us. "Paddy and I bought a home here last month because we decided to settle down and live here year-round. We're officially retired, you know, but Paddy still takes an occasional temp job. I think he gets too bored, otherwise. He really loved working in collections, if you can imagine that. I thought working here at Quinta Mazatlan would be a good way for me to meet people, too. We've moved around so much during our marriage, that I've never really had the chance to connect with neighbors, so I'm really looking forward to it."

She handed Luce our bag. I was ready to make a run for it to escape Poppy's life story—I could feel it coming—but Luce smiled at the woman, and I knew what that meant.

Poppy was going to keep talking.

"I love the MOB," Poppy went on, "but sometimes I just don't want to talk about birds, you know? And now that the SpaceX project is underway, there are all kinds of new people moving into the area. Morning, Regina!" She waved at a woman who passed by in the hallway beyond the store.

Poppy leaned her elbows on the counter and removed her glasses from her nose.

"Really," she told us, "it's just so sad that Birdy won't see the fruits of all his labor to get SpaceX up and running down here. He's brought so much hope to the region. You know, a lot of people associated this area with drug smuggling and illegal immigration, but now, the Valley will have a whole new bright future as a spaceport. People flying in space just for fun—people like you and me! I'd be thrilled beyond words to be on that first flight, wouldn't you? Imagine that!"

"I don't know if I can," I said, because my imagination was already busy trying to figure out a way to make a graceful exit from Poppy's conversational clutches. "I'm so new to Texas, I'm still getting over not seeing cowboys and herds of longhorns everywhere. The whole citrus festival thing was enough of a surprise to me—I always thought of Florida, not Texas, when it came to oranges."

"No kidding? And we have such wonderful citrus around here. The valley used to be filled with orchards. Speaking of which, you are coming to the parade on Saturday, right?" Poppy asked us as I edged Luce toward the store door. "We can always use last minute help with the float, you know. And I'm not sure who's going to be wearing our kiskadee outfit this year. You two are both so tall, maybe you'd be willing? You'd make great kiskadees!"

Poppy laughed, apparently delighted with her word choice. "Oh, my. Great Kiskadees! Get it? Our signature kiskadee is a Great Kiskadee!"

"I'm sure we'll be there," Luce replied, waving goodbye. "Tell Paddy hello for us."

She tucked her hand around my arm and steered me out of the mansion.

"She sure likes to talk," Luce commented. "I wonder if Paddy used to get so immersed in his work that she never felt like she had anyone to talk to. He seems like a jovial kind of guy, but if he was into curating museum collections, maybe he wasn't a very good conversationalist while he was working. "

"Or maybe he just got used to tuning her out," I suggested. "She can really get going when she wants to."

We walked back down the beautifully landscaped walk to the main driveway leading to the parking lot. The sky was blue and the sun shone brightly. Along the walk, cacti mixed with mesquite and a host of other native plants from which issued a variety of chirping and cheeping calls of hidden birds. Plain Chachalacas scooted around under the trees, while a continuous stream of visitors made their leisurely way up the drive, many of them stopping to take photos of the towering date palm trees and the occasional Great Kiskadee or Inca Dove that posed obligingly in the nearest trees.

The place was a playground paradise for birders and photographers. No wonder Quinta Mazatlan received thousands of visitors every year.

"I bet that moving around a lot was probably hard on Poppy," Luce speculated, obviously still thinking about her conversational exchange with Paddy's wife. "Maybe she's never had close friends as a result, and that's why she just dives in and starts talking. And talking."

"I think we should introduce her to Chief Pacheco, and she can talk to him," I said. "She told me she thinks Mark is doing drugs."

Luce slowed her step and turned to face me.

"Why would she say that to you?" she asked. "We don't know Mark, and even if we did, it's none of our business. That's more than just talking. That's malicious gossip."

I opened the car door for her, and she got in. I understood, and agreed with, what she said about Poppy speaking badly about Mark. It was inappropriate and none of our business.

At the same time, I couldn't help wondering if Poppy's speculation might help connect some dots on the way to solving Birdy's murder. In particular, I was still thinking about Mark's comment to the Boston birder about how well he knew the hidden spots in Estero Llano. If Poppy's suspicion that Mark was involved with drugs was true, might he also be involved in some illegal drug activity?

Illegal activity that Birdy Johnson might have unknowingly interrupted during his regular Wednesday morning birding walk?

I couldn't forget how green Mark had grown at the reminder of Birdy's death just a short while ago. I'd attributed it to belated remorse over his thoughtless comments to his grieving uncle, but what if that remorse was . . . guilt?

Did Mark know something about Birdy's death that no one else knew?

Could Mark himself have killed his uncle's best friend?

"Gossip or not, Luce," I said to my wife as I slid into my car seat and started the engine, "I'm telling the chief about it. Eddie's not the only one at risk here, remember. We've got a nameless note writer to worry about. The more leads I can pass along to Pacheco, the faster he'll solve his case, and then I won't have to keep checking for cars tailing us all the way back home to Minnesota."

"You think trouble might follow us home?" Luce asked. "But the note writer wants us to leave. You know—what happens in Texas, stays in Texas."

"That sounds like a line from a country-western song." I exited the parking lot and turned right, back towards downtown McAllen. "I need some coffee. And doughnuts. I hope this place where we're meeting the chief has both because I have the feeling it's going to be a very long day."

Out of the corner of my eye, I noticed that Luce was downloading the directions on her phone to our rendezvous with Chief Pacheco.

"The name of the place is Shipley Do-nuts," she told me. "And every review I'm seeing here raves about the doughnuts, especially the glazed ones. Nothing about coffee, but I've never seen a doughnut shop that didn't have coffee."

"And birders for customers," I added. "Doughnuts are one of the five food groups for birders, you know."

"And for policemen," Luce added.

"Absolutely," I agreed, laughing. "Did I ever tell you about the time a patrolman stopped me on the highway and I offered him a doughnut . . . ?"

Chapter Fifteen

Sure enough, as soon as we stepped into Shipley Do-nuts, we recognized a birder we'd met last night at the float construction. He was just leaving with a box of doughnuts, and after a quick hello, he hustled back out to the parking lot, leaving us with a panoramic view of more varieties of doughnuts than I'd ever seen in one place.

My mouth started watering in anticipation.

"No wonder there's a line of cars at both of their drive-up windows," Luce remarked as she stood transfixed in front of the loaded racks of pastries that stood behind the counter. "I didn't think a shop like this existed anywhere anymore. There have got to be at least sixty different varieties of doughnuts in here."

She looked beyond the metal racks to the bustling open kitchen space on our left where a team of four workers was mixing and cutting dough, sliding trays in and out of fryers, injecting doughnuts with creamy fillings, and dipping doughnut tops in frostings and toppings.

"Hand-cut," Luce breathed in awe. "These doughnuts are all hand cut."

"Can I help you?" asked the Hispanic woman behind the counter after passing a box of doughnuts to her coworker at the drive-up window. Her dark hair was tucked up into a Shipley Do-nut ball cap and her white apron had smudges of pink and chocolate frosting on it. Beside the register was a stack of flat boxes, all marked with the red-and-white Shipley Do-Nut logo that matched the tall street sign outside the shop. I thought that *The Greatest Name in Do-Nuts* emblazoned on the sign was setting a pretty high standard, but one whiff of the doughnuts inside the shop convinced me that whoever made the sign knew what he was talking about.

This was doughnut heaven.

"Yes, please," I said to the cashier. "We'll take a half-dozen."

I began reeling off my selections of doughnuts, with Luce adding in her choices when I hesitated. A moment later, we sat down at one of the round, brown tables in front of the bright red half-wall that separated the seating from the open work area, a box of six different doughnuts in my hands and two big cups of coffee in Luce's.

"This place is a real find," Luce said, opening the box and letting her hand hover over the doughnuts, trying to decide which of the warm, fragrant delicacies would be her first taste of a Shipley Do-nut.

"Hey, Bob! Luce!"

Chief Pacheco waved to us from the counter, where he was ordering his own half-dozen doughnuts. I could hear him speaking in Spanish to the woman who worked the counter, and he called a greeting to several of the kitchen workers as he carried his order to the table to join us.

"Looks like you've been here before," I commented as the chief sat down.

"Are you kidding?" he smiled. "We have standing orders with Shipley for staff meetings. Not to mention that I know everyone who works here. I spent a couple summers cutting doughnuts myself when I was in high school."

"These are to die for," Luce said, wiping a crumb of a Bavarian filled doughnut off her lip with a slender finger.

I nudged her foot under the table. "Luce," I said, rolling my eyes in the chief's direction.

She looked at me and then at the chief.

I could see Pacheco trying hard not to smile at my wife's choice of words.

"Oh," she said, wiping her lips with a napkin, a light blush of pink rising on her cheeks. "Sorry. Maybe not the best thing to say right now. How about . . . they're amazing."

Pacheco let his smile spread across his face. When he did that, I could see a startling family resemblance to his mother and niece. I'd thought Rosalie and Pearl were both beauties; now I realized

Pacheco was probably what most women would consider a very handsome man. In fact, if he'd been a faculty member at Savage High School, I had a sneaking suspicion I would have probably been spending a good portion of my forty-hour work week dealing with teenage girls' crushes on that good-looking Mr. Pacheco.

Thank God for small favors.

The chief picked up our conversation where it had been before Luce's ill-timed turn of phrase.

"The company is a great employer, too," he said. "Shipley is a Texas company, founded in 1936, and they've had loyal customers for generations. Most of the workers here stay on the job for ten years because they like it so well. We're big on digging in around here, in case you haven't noticed—Texans stick together, for the most part."

His last words struck a chord in me, and I instantly recalled the tension I'd sensed between Rosalie and Buzz Davis yesterday morning on the park deck when Buzz made his veiled remark about immigrants. He'd struck a nerve with Rosalie, and now that I knew about her daughter and son-in-law's situation, I could understand why.

"Are you referring to the debate about illegal immigrants around here?" I asked.

Pacheco's face clouded.

Crap.

I gave myself a mental head slap.

My mouth had run ahead of my mind, and my foot had jumped right in it. Rosalie's self-exiled daughter was Pacheco's sister.

Way to go, Bob. Remind the nice chief of his own family heartache.

"I'm sorry." It was my turn to apologize. "Forget I said that. Let's start over. How's Eddie doing this morning?"

Pacheco took a bite out of one of his glazed raised doughnuts and chewed slowly, keeping his eyes on me the whole time.

"No, let's clear the air here, first," he said. "Yes, illegal immigration is an issue for all of us who live in this part of Texas, but you have to remember, it's nothing new to us, either. The Lower Rio

Grande Valley has a history of border control problems, and many families have members on both sides of the border. It's a fact of life here. We deal with it."

He took a gulp of his coffee and set the cup back down. He tipped his head in the direction of the workers in the open kitchen.

"As you can see, our population is filled with Americans of Hispanic descent. Hispanic culture has shaped the area, and it's one of the reasons this strip of towns along the border is growing so fast. People come here on vacation and then move here to live. We've got nice weather, a blend of cultures, great restaurants, a laid-back lifestyle, and low taxes."

"And birds," Luce reminded him. "Ecotourism is a booming industry around here from what we see."

Pacheco nodded. "Believe me, we like that it is, and we want to keep it that way. But every growing area has its headaches, and illegal immigration happens to be the one that we can't make go away."

"But I thought Eddie was here to work on improving border control," Luce remarked. "If you want to improve something, doesn't that mean the current method isn't working as well as you want it to?"

Pacheco finished one of his doughnuts and picked up another.

"The drone project has been in development for a lot longer than people realize," he explained. "Personally, I don't think it's the best way to find illegals trying to cross the border. It picks up heat signatures, and we have a lot of wildlife around here, so we end up tracking animals, instead of people. I'm sure the US Fish and Wildlife Service appreciates our effort because we can provide them with a lot of data they wouldn't otherwise get, but it's not solving any immigration problems."

I snatched the chocolate-iced doughnut out of our box before Luce could grab it. With a look of mild reprimand, she took the coconut-topped one that was left.

"What Eddie—who, by the way, is doing fine this morning and back at the border control offices—is working on is a hush-hush drone program that targets drug runners using some new technology

I don't even pretend to understand," Pacheco continued. "And because it's got high security, most folks don't know that it's about drugs. As a result, our local community that works with illegal immigrants is convinced it's a new program targeting illegals, and it's got them upset, which translates into one more big headache for me."

"Your mother, Rosalie," I guessed. "She's a part of that local community that advocates for new immigrants."

The chief nodded. "Every time I see her for the past month, she reams me up one side and down the other for being insensitive to the plight of illegals. I thought Birdy would set her straight since he was working on the drones with Eddie, but my mother . . ."

His voice trailed off in frustration, and he shook his head.

"She's very stubborn," he said, "and hot-tempered. I think Birdy took great pleasure in teasing her. It wouldn't surprise me if he refused to give her the details about the drone just to see her get angry."

I slid a look at my wife. I'd been known to push her a little too far with teasing, myself. Generally, that resulted in me apologizing and her letting me make it up to her with gift cards to her favorite massage salons.

I wondered how Birdy made up with Rosalie when he teased her too much.

A fancy night out?

Flowers and chocolates?

Finding a park rarity?

Buzz's comment came roaring back to me. He'd said that was why Birdy had headed to Alligator Lake yesterday morning—to find a park rarity for Rosalie. I'd assumed he'd meant a rare bird, but now I wondered . . .

"Does the border control keep records of what the drones find?" I asked Pacheco.

The chief finished his coffee and set the empty cup down.

"You'd have to ask Eddie," he said. "It's not my program."

"Why?" Luce asked me, folding the top over to close our empty box. I could see suspicion in her eyes. "What are you thinking?"

I gave her a smile and turned to address the chief.

"I have something to show you," I said, pulling both the threatening note and the fabric shred from my pocket.

He took them both and read the note.

"I found it taped on our guest suite door very early this morning," I told him before he could ask. "And the material is a shred the dog found near the wall where I think our note-writer exited the yard. I don't know if it's from the intruder, but the dog seemed really pleased when she brought it to me."

"You didn't tell me you had that," Luce said, a hint of annoyance in her voice. "The dog brought you a scrap?"

She turned to Pacheco. "Can I see that?"

He handed it to her.

Luce fingered the cloth for a moment.

"Do you recognize it?" I asked her.

"From what?" My wife didn't sound annoyed anymore.

That was a good thing.

Except that now, she sounded really ticked off, instead.

That was not a good thing.

In fact, I got the feeling that if Pacheco hadn't been seated across the table from us, my wife would have read me the riot act for failing to share the material scrap with her. Luce never liked it when I withheld information from her, even when I thought it was best for her not to know. As a husband, I took my marital responsibility to protect my wife very seriously, but Luce insisted that she could take care of herself just fine and that I needed to chuck my outdated perspective of women as the gentler sex.

On the other hand, if anyone delighted in being spoiled with spa certificates or world-class chocolates, it was my wife. A smart husband remembers those kinds of things . . . which led me to wonder if there was a really good massage place in McAllen where I could get Luce an appointment for this afternoon.

I had a feeling we were both going to need it after this particular instance of my not sharing information with her.

"Anywhere," I prompted her, trying to move her past my glaring sin of omission and into the realm of brilliant collaboration. "Does the print look familiar at all?"

She flashed me another angry look before studying the little bit of fabric more closely, and then I watched understanding spreading over her features.

Hooray. Maybe I was going to get away with my protective instincts after all.

"It's a floral print, like the Hawaiian shirt Schooner was wearing yesterday."

The chief's attention zeroed in on the fabric.

"A lot of people wear prints like that around here," he said.

"But a lot of people don't know that Luce and I are staying at the Birds Nest or that we're from Minnesota," I countered. "And Schooner isn't the only one with a shirt like this. Mark," I said, then realized I didn't even know his last name, "Buzz's great-nephew, he was wearing a shirt like this when he birded with us this morning at Quinta Mazatlan. And guess what?"

Luce and the chief both looked at me.

"Mark's shirt had a rip in it, like a piece had torn off."

Pacheco's eyes returned to the fabric scrap in Luce's fingers.

"I think I'll just take this with me," he said, plucking the little strip of material from my wife's fingertips and carefully tucking it into his own shirt's chest pocket.

"I guess I'm going to have to take a ride over to Quinta Mazatlan and have a word with Mark, then," he added, closing the top flap on the box of his remaining doughnuts.

"His last name is Myers, by the way," the chief said. "I should know—the kid's been picked up so much for disorderly conduct that I should probably offer him a punch card. The only reason he's not in jail or rehab is because his uncle is so well connected around here. Buzz Davis generally has a knack for getting what he wants, I've noticed."

"Like the SpaceX installation down here?" Luce asked.

Pacheco gave her an appraising glance. "Sharp lady. Yes. I'm sure you've picked up some of the static around here surrounding the project. There isn't a birder along the Rio Grande Valley who doesn't have an opinion about it, and it's generally not a good one."

"So we've gathered," Luce said. "Cynnie Scott was at Buzz's place last night and she spelled out for us what some of the ecological consequences of SpaceX could mean for the area."

The chief sat back in his chair. "Cynnie Scott is a force to be reckoned with. The woman is unstoppable when it comes to promoting ecotourism, which means she has the support of all our ecotourism businesses in the Valley. But if you're a SpaceX advocate, she's the enemy. For the longest time, I thought she was going to single-handedly keep the project out of Bocha Chica, thanks to her appeals to every conservation group in America to intervene. But the project got the green light after all."

Which, I knew from our conversation with her last night, did not make Cynnie Scott happy. As I recalled, the naturalist had said that she was going to be continuing to work against the SpaceX project, using a more personal approach. What that might entail would be pure conjecture on my part, since she hadn't provided us with any details.

Not that I was any stranger to conjecture. I happened to like conjecture very much. I did it a lot.

I just happened to know that conjecture very frequently turned out to be wrong, if not downright stupid.

And stupid was not something I was fond of being, which was one of the reasons I asked so many questions.

"By the way," I said, asking another of those questions that had recently popped into my head, "what exactly does Buzz Davis have to do with Space X?"

Pacheco leaned forward again, sliding his elbows onto the table. "What do you mean?"

"I've seen clippings and overheard people talking about the spaceport," I explained, "and I know he and Birdy were in a parade about it, but aside from his past involvement with the space program, I don't know what his connection is to it. He's not running the project, is he?"

Pacheco tapped twice on his box of doughnuts. "The land," he said. "The tract of land in Boca Chica, where they're going to build SpaceX, belongs to Buzz. Or, at least, it did. It belongs to SpaceX now."

I let out a low whistle.

"I guess that explains the Porsche in his garage," I commented to Luce.

"And maybe Mark's classic Mustang, too," she said.

"Cynnie Scott must be furious with him," I speculated. "Buzz enabled SpaceX to site its installation in a critical ecological area, and yet he's a member of the MOB. And she's the group president."

"She was at Buzz's last night, working on the float," Luce pointed out. "Given the SpaceX deal, I expect their relationship is . . . conflicted . . . to put it mildly, though I didn't see any direct evidence of that. They seemed cordial enough around each other. In fact, I think I remember Cynnie giving Buzz a hard time about taking too long to let her know about the Eared Grebe he'd found that morning, before . . . ah . . . Birdy . . ." She let the sentence trail off.

I patted her hand. Finding bodies together was not one of the things I promised her when we got married, but it seems to happen every so often. On the upside, one of the best things about being married to another birder, I've discovered, was that Luce had the same memory for details I did, so if I missed something, I could generally depend on her having caught it. That was a big plus when we were trying to identify a bird unfamiliar to us; Luce was an ace at picking up minor field marks.

She was also an ace at picking up what I was thinking, which could be either a plus or minus, depending on what I was thinking. When she could jump right onto my train of thought about chasing a bird, that was great. When she figured out that I hadn't only forgotten we had tickets to the symphony but was hoping she'd forget, too—not so great.

"I think they've made their peace," Chief Pacheco said, referring to Cynnie and Buzz's opposing positions on SpaceX. "Besides, money talks. I'm sure Cynnie likes the money Buzz contributes to the club, even though she hates where it might be coming from, as in the sale of his land for the construction of a spaceport. When you have no other option, you learn to make accommodations, even if you still don't quite forgive."

Pacheco's cell phone rang, and he removed it from his belt holder, checked the number, then slid it back into its case.

"Speaking of accommodations, are you two heading back to Minnesota today?" Pacheco asked.

"We're leaving after the Citrus Festival Parade on Saturday," Luce told him. "I've got a soft spot for parades."

"And your niece Pearl told us it was worth sticking around for," I added. "I don't want to disappoint the Queen. It's not every day I get an invitation from royalty."

Pacheco didn't look pleased. "Eddie's no longer a suspect, if you're worrying about him getting arrested. But your threatening note writer—that's another matter we'll have to try to track down. Given the timing, my guess is that it has something to do with Birdy's murder, unless you've been going around town deliberately antagonizing the locals."

He gave me and Luce a questioning glance.

"You haven't been doing that, have you?"

We assured him we'd been Minnesota nice to everyone we'd met in the Valley.

"Well, somebody doesn't want you around, obviously," he said, patting the pocket where he'd stowed the note. "Do me a favor and be careful, okay? I'd ask you to stay away from any of the MOB, but I guess that's just about impossible since they're all over the place down here, and you're here to bird."

The chief stood up and tucked the box of remaining doughnuts under his arm.

"I'll check in with Rhonda and let her know I'm going to make sure she's got some extra patrolmen on duty in her neighborhood around the Birds Nest until you leave town," he said. "If anything else comes up I should know about, you've got my phone number."

He waved to the crew back in the kitchen and left us to figure out our plans for the rest of the day.

"Where to next?" Luce asked, stifling a yawn. "You want to try the Santa Ana National Wildlife Refuge? Someone told me they had a Tropical Parula there the other day."

"Let's do that tomorrow morning," I suggested. "We'll have better luck earlier in the day is my guess." I looked at my wife's face and noticed shadows beginning to show under her eyes.

"Would you be up for a nap? Or down, as the case may be? You look tired," I quickly added when she began to object. "And you weren't feeling your best yesterday, as I recall. Besides, I want to go talk to Eddie about the drones, and I know you're not that interested in them. What do you say? You can nap, I'll hang out with Eddie, we'll have a late lunch, then go see the parrots flock in Weslaco."

Luce yawned again. "I am kind of tired," she conceded. "I think it's our schedule here. I'm not used to sleeping in and staying up late. Those aren't a morning chef's hours."

I stood up and put out my hand to my wife. "Let's go, then. We'll get you tucked in for a nap, and I'll go bug Eddie."

Although bugging Eddie wasn't exactly what I had in mind.

What I really wanted was for Eddie to educate me about bugging . . . via a drone.

Chapter Sixteen

So, are there recordings of what the drones sense during their flights over the border?" I asked Eddie about an hour later in his temporary work space in an annex adjacent to the National Guard Armory in Weslaco.

"Do you want the short answer or the long one?" he asked me. He was sitting in front of a console with about a hundred dials and registers. On the other side of the console was a long table covered with electronic parts that apparently belonged to the dissected drone that sat on another table nearby.

"Short would be nice," I said. I pointed at his tropical print shirt. "What is it with the Hawaiian print shirts around here? I'm beginning to think it's like an unofficial birder uniform."

Eddie laughed and removed his reading glasses from their perch on the end of his nose.

"It's a happy shirt," he said. "Everyone down here is happy to be here where it's warm, instead of somewhere up north where it's freezing. Use it or lose it, Bob."

As soon as I had walked in and seen Eddie's shirt, I'd made a memo to me for later to tell Chief Pacheco to forget about the fabric cloth that Maddie the Labrador had retrieved for me. If the chief wanted to question everyone along the Lower Rio Grande Valley who had a tropical print shirt, he was going to need a task force of thousands.

Clearly, the scrap of material was not the most efficient or helpful lead I'd ever come up with. I'd be better off searching for a needle in a haystack than trying to find whose Hawaiian shirt left a shred in the Birds Nest's yard.

The Birds Nest.

I gave myself a mental kick in the head.

Rhonda's backyard, the backyard she shared with the Birds Nest guest suite, was home to all kinds of birds and their nests. Anyone who had ever watched a bird build a nest knew birds were masters of ingenuity, using a multitude of materials for their construction projects; depending on the species, you could find nests made of yarn and twigs, dental floss and animal fur, mud and saliva, snakeskin and cotton. With all the nesting activity in Rhonda's yard, I should have been surprised there weren't stacks of fabric scraps lying around as nesting supplies flown in by the birds themselves as they cruised the neighborhood for suitable materials.

For all we knew, that shred I'd given to Pacheco had been on its way to decorate a bird nursery, and not left as evidence of an unwelcome intruder.

Hopefully, my current idea for a lead would turn out to be more helpful.

"The short answer is yes," Eddie answered, "we have records, but Bob, you've got to understand this is still a developing technology. We don't have total coverage of an area. The drones are moving all the time, so unless something happens right under them, we don't know about it. It's luck, not skill."

"But you're focusing on the border area, right? You've got to have some drones along the Rio Grande, and that would include some of the park areas, since the river is so close by," I reasoned. "Eddie, if you've got any records on Estero Llano Grande State Park, even for the last few weeks, can't we just take a look at them?"

Eddie stroked his long white beard and then reached over to toggle a switch back and forth on his console. "Let me ask you something," he said. "What do you think you're going to find in a drone report?"

I poked a finger in Eddie's tropical-shirt-covered chest.

"Evidence," I said, "of why Birdy Johnson was at Alligator Lake."

Eddie leaned back on his chair and studied me. "But like I just said, it's luck, not skill," he repeated. "We don't have 24/7 surveillance capability."

"I know," I assured him. "I'm not looking for the moment Birdy was killed. I'm looking to see whatever you can show me that moved around Alligator Lake in the day before he was killed."

Eddie finally gave up trying to dissuade me and hit some buttons on his console. Three small screens lit up in front of him.

"Well, then, Bob, you must be one of the luckiest son-of-a-guns on the planet," Eddie said, adjusting a dial, "because it just so happens that Alligator Lake is directly under the path of one of the drones I was testing for Birdy."

A spark of excitement ran down my spine. How lucky was that?

Or, maybe, not lucky at all, but planned.

"Did Birdy set up these aerial routes for the drone?" I asked Eddie, my excitement growing.

Eddie fiddled with another dial and the image on the screen took on sharper definition.

"Yes," he said, "he did."

I placed a hand on the back of Eddie's chair and leaned in to get a better look at the screen. "And did he give you any explanation of why he chose the route he did?"

Eddie was quiet for a moment or two.

"He said that Rosalie's favorite place at Estero Llano was Alligator Lake because that was where he'd first met her on a birding trip years ago."

I tried to piece together my thoughts about the personal significance of Alligator Lake to Rosalie and Birdy and the fact that he'd told Buzz he was heading there to look for a park rarity for Rosalie the morning he was killed. I still wasn't sure how it would help catch Birdy's killer, but I had the nagging feeling the scene of the crime was the key to Birdy's murder.

"Eddie," I said, "did Birdy ever talk to you about his relationship with Rosalie? I mean, would he have mentioned to you if they'd had a quarrel, or if he was in the doghouse with her, because of the work he was doing with the drone surveillance?"

Eddie started to object, but I cut him off.

"I know," I assured him. "The drone surveillance isn't about illegal immigrants. It's about drug smuggling. But Rosalie didn't know that, right?"

Eddie stroked his beard a few more times.

"No. I'm pretty sure that Birdy wouldn't have told her any details about what we're doing here. The Border Patrol generally likes to keep this kind of development project under wraps until they've got all the kinks worked out."

He rested his hands on his thighs. "Now that you mention it, Birdy did seem a little smug the last time I saw him, which was the night before he was killed. Smug, like he had a secret."

Eddie shut his eyes, and I wondered if he was replaying a conversation in his head since his face took on a series of expressions: a smile, a frown, the raised eyebrows of surprise, and another smile. His eyes opened then and he immediately peered at the monitor screen, which showed five glowing spots arranged in a flattened X shape.

"That goofy old Romeo," Eddie said, tracing a shape on top of the glowing spots. "He was at Alligator Lake to finish off his heart."

Finish his heart?

"Birdy Johnson had heart disease?" I asked, totally confused.

Eddie guffawed.

"No, Bob," he said when he stopped laughing. "Birdy Johnson was using his drone to set up a special valentine for Rosalie. Look."

I watched as he traced a shape over the spots. What I had taken to be a flat X was, under Eddie's outlining finger, the top half of a heart. He pointed to an empty spot a little ways beneath the center of the X.

"Right here," Eddie said. "This is where you found Birdy, on the southern shore of Alligator Lake. You put another heat source there, and it makes the bottom point of a heart shape. A valentine. Valentine's Day is only a few weeks away. About two weeks ago, Rosalie was here one afternoon in the shop, and she was giving Birdy an earful about immigration reform."

Eddie traced the heart shape on the screen one more time.

"That Rosalie—she's got a temper on her, I think," he commented. "A regular spit-fire. Anyway, after she left, I remember Birdy looking sort of hang-dog, and he said something about how he'd better come up with a rarity for her for Valentine's Day to get back on her good side."

By golly, I was right. Birdy made up with Rosalie by finding rare birds for her.

I love it when I'm right.

And I was right about the location being important in Birdy's murder, too.

Though I never would have guessed that the location was important because he was using it to create a love note.

I'd thought it had something to do with the border, as in illegal immigrants sneaking over it, or drug runners using the spot for an exchange.

Remember what I said about conjecture?

Now, thanks to Eddie's drone records, I knew why Birdy was alone at Alligator Lake when he was killed.

He was building a valentine.

Why someone would object to that enough to kill him—and who that someone was—was still up in the air.

Unfortunately, no drone records could give me that answer.

"You want to see the Weslaco parrot flock tonight?" Eddie asked. "It's kind of like a wild goose chase, driving from spot to spot where you think they are, except that you actually do find them eventually. Of course, they're not geese, either."

He paused and scratched his upper lip.

"So maybe it's not really like a wild goose chase, I guess."

I patted Crazy Eddie on his shoulder. "We're planning on it," I told him. "Luce is resting up right now so we can go. She's having a hard time on this trip," I confided. "She's so used to her early morning work shift, it's hard for her to adjust to late mornings and irregular meals. I never realized how much she was a creature of habit, I guess."

Eddie turned off his screens and toggled a few more switches.

"We're all creatures of habit, Bob," he said. "It's just that some habits are good and some are bad. For instance," he said, leaning back in his chair and lacing his fingers together over his ample belly, "you have a habit of finding bodies when you go birding. That's probably a bad habit. On the other hand, I can't look at any kind of electronic gizmo without thinking of a way to improve it. That's a good habit. I think," he added. "Though my wife wasn't too thrilled that time I tried to rewire her curling iron to heat it faster. I liked the really short haircut she had to get afterwards, though."

I looked at the blank screens on the console.

"And people close to us get to know our habits," I continued, thinking about Birdy's ill-fated valentine attempt to give Rosalie a rarity she didn't expect to find. His gesture of reconciliation had ended with his death.

Wow. I knew making amends with a woman could be hard, but I didn't know it could be murder. Something to keep in mind, I supposed.

"Hold on," I said, a detail from a conversation bubbling up from my memory. "Buzz and Birdy were at Estero Llano every Wednesday morning checking for species. Rosalie said so. Every birder in the MOB would know their routine, right?"

Eddie nodded slowly. "I suppose so. The MOB seem a pretty tight crew. From what I've seen while I've been here, they're always sharing bird sightings on their phones. It's not like some birders I've known, who try to keep sightings of rare birds to themselves."

The idea of habit and routine began to dance around in my head in relation to Birdy's murder. "So if he'd been out setting up the sensors on Wednesday mornings, a birder who'd seen him do that on a previous Wednesday morning would know when he could catch Birdy alone," I theorized.

Eddie moved his hands back to his console and sat upright again in his chair.

"Give me a minute," he said, a hint of excitement in his voice. "You just gave me an idea."

He proceeded to flip another section of switches and tapped on a different set of keys on the console. A wider screen lit up before him and I realized he was looking at the rear ends of a row of cars in a parking lot.

"The parking lot is Estero Llano's," he explained. "I set up a tiny video camera system to monitor the cars that parked. That's why I was there yesterday morning—I was fine-tuning it. Marci—she's the park superintendent—asked me if I could help them gauge how many visitors weren't paying the admission fee once they got to the park registration area, since their receipts seemed lower than their visitor count. Visitors are supposed to register their vehicles when they pay, so she wanted to know how many vehicles didn't match up to paid registrations."

He hit one more key and the license plates came into clear focus.

"This is the parking lot Wednesday morning," he said. "Let's see which of the MOB might have arrived early enough to commit a murder. The chief already checked all the security tapes for the park's perimeter, and no one was trespassing into the park that morning, so the murderer must have walked right in the front entrance."

He started the recording at daybreak when the park opened, and stopped it every time someone arrived, so we could get a look at the face. We hit the jackpot about fifteen minutes after sunrise.

"Birdy and Buzz," Crazy Eddie said as the two men climbed out of the same green Porsche I'd seen in Buzz's garage. A moment later, I picked out Schooner and Gunnar getting out of a SUV with a Minnesota license plate, followed by Paddy Mac and his wife Poppy exiting a sedan, a small knapsack in her hand.

"No surprises there," I said. "Poppy, Paddy, Schooner and Gunnar were with me when I spotted the body, and I met Buzz on the park deck before I headed over to Alligator Lake, where he told us Birdy had gone."

Eddie continued to run the recording until I saw a classic Mustang roar into the lot and slide into a parking slot.

"Slow down!" I said. "I think I'm going to know this one."

Eddie slowed the recording until a young man stepped from the car. He turned his head, scanning the parking lot and then the camera caught his face clearly.

On the monitor, Mark Myers looked downright frantic.

"It's Mark," I confirmed. "Buzz's nephew. He was there yesterday morning."

I blew out a breath, unsure how I felt about the discovery, especially since I'd already dismissed the floral scrap that had led me to suspect Mark's involvement in Birdy's murder as a worthless clue. I looked again at the slow-moving image of Buzz's nephew. "What was he doing there?"

The truth was that I'd come to . . . well, not exactly *like* Mark . . . but at least feel some compassion for the kid after our birding walk. Sure, he had some pressing and very difficult personal issues to work through, but my gut told me he was a good kid. The possibility that our shared passion for birds could blind me to the true nature of a person was disturbing. Combined with my just-revealed inability to recognize my own wife's need for routine, I was suddenly doubtful of what I'd always believed was one of my unique strengths: a hyper-sensitivity to others and the surroundings in which I found myself.

It was one of the main reasons I loved birding so much: I prided myself on close attention to the little details that allowed me to identify one bird from another. That knowledge, that gift of acute observation, made me feel like I had a special connection to nature itself, almost as if nature waited patiently to reveal its mysteries to me. It was, I believed, what made me a good high school counselor, too—I was able to synthesize careful observation with knowledge and sensitivity to help my students find their way in the world, even on the occasions when the world wasn't such a welcoming place for them to be.

If I couldn't trust my own abilities, my own gut, where did that leave me as a birder or counselor?

Gutless?

Or just tragically mistaken?

"Well, whatever he was doing, he wasn't killing Birdy," Eddie said, breaking into my wallow of self-doubt. "Heck, he wasn't there long enough to write down his license plate number, let alone get to Alligator Lake, commit a murder, and get back to the parking lot."

I focused on the screen, which showed Mark getting back into the Mustang within minutes after his arrival. His face looked angry. He pulled out of his parking space and zoomed out of the camera's range, but not before I saw him thump the wheel of his Mustang in what looked like intense frustration.

Mark hadn't killed Birdy.

My gut was right.

Which meant that I was not, after all, gutless.

Or even tragically mistaken, hopefully.

I supposed it did mean, however, that I might have just a tiny inclination to overreact.

Imagine that.

The other thing I tried to imagine was what Mustang Mark was doing at Estero Llano for just those few minutes on Wednesday morning.

Something had upset him.

As in, really upset him.

And then last night, Mark had been so drunk, he'd almost hit Luce in Buzz's driveway before he announced to everyone there that, despite appearances, his uncle hated Birdy.

For a moment, the wheels in my head spun crazily and landed on something I'd noticed last night.

Buzz Davis had been exceptionally stoic about Birdy's death, to the point that he was driving a lift truck around with citrus to help build a float.

If I were grieving the death of a best friend, I don't know that I could drive a toy truck across a carpet, let alone a lift truck that required precision and concentration.

Mark's accusation of his uncle came back to me: he said his uncle hated Birdy Johnson and that he was a two-faced liar.

Why would Mark say that? Why would he think Buzz had hated his long-time friend?

And if it were true, could Buzz Davis not only be a popular ex-astronaut and a very rich man, but a man who had held a grudge for years until he could get away with murder?

Payback, Mark said.

A very drunk Mark who clearly took Birdy's death very hard.

And why was that? What kind of connection was there between Mark and Birdy?

"Stick me with a fork," I told Eddie. "I'm done. It seems like for every question your records can answer, they raise ten more. People who solve murders for a living must feel like they spend half their time on merry-go-rounds."

I supposed that someone could probably say the same of birders like me—we spin our wheels chasing birds all over the map, sometimes for years. But at least at the end of a birding chase, we get to add a bird to our life list.

When you solve a murder, on the other hand, you find a killer, but it doesn't bring anyone back to life.

Chapter Seventeen

Given our experience the night before at the vulture roost, Eddie and I decided he'd bow out of joining Luce and me to watch the parrots flocking in Weslaco at sunset.

"I'm going to get enough grief from my wife for one gunshot graze," he explained. "No way I'm looking for two. Besides," he said, "I promised Chief Pacheco I'd stay out of sight for forty-eight hours to give him time to investigate my shooting without having to worry about me landing back in someone's crosshairs. I've got a room and a bodyguard here at the base till further notice, courtesy of the chief."

"Aha," I said, "that must be the reason there's a very grim young man with an Army-issued gun standing outside your office door here. By the way," I confided in Eddie, "I don't think he has much of a sense of humor. When I told him he could pat me down if necessary, but that I'm ticklish, he didn't even crack a smile."

Eddie waved me out of his office. "Get out of here, birdbrain. Go get your wife and seek out some of your own kind."

I decided to take the scenic route back to McAllen from Weslaco, so I stayed off Highway 83 and wound through residential and commercial neighborhoods that took me from the Armory through the towns of Donna, Alamo, San Juan, and Pharr back to the Birds Nest. As I drove, I replayed in my head what I'd seen on Eddie's surveillance recordings, and tried to glean from them whatever information I could that might shed some light on Birdy's murder.

The fact that we had visual evidence that Mark was not inside the park prior to Birdy's murder eliminated him as a murder suspect, though I still wondered what had happened to make him so angry as he tore out of the parking lot.

Why would he have been there at all, if he was gone again so quickly?

I ran through a list of reasons I would drive somewhere specific, then turn around and leave within minutes.

Maybe I had laundry to drop off or pick up. That would be a quick turn-around.

Maybe I was supposed to meet someone, then realized I was at the wrong place, or had the wrong time. I'd be back in the car in no time.

Maybe I wanted to surprise someone, but then learned they weren't coming. No reason to stick around in that case.

My mind continued to remix possibilities.

Maybe I was going to surprise someone by showing up unexpectedly with someone else . . . kind of like the boy who shows up at Prom with a hot date after his girlfriend dumped him at the last minute to go with some other boy.

But Mark was alone in the parking lot, and he wasn't wearing a tux, so I scratched the hot date/revenge scenario from my list, although . . .

What if Mark had planned to surprise someone who he knew would be in the parking lot . . . like his uncle Buzz and Birdy, who everyone knew came to the park on Wednesday mornings . . . but when he got there and saw they'd already arrived and gone into the park . . . he left?

Why would he leave, and not try to find them? On the recording, Mark looked angry and frustrated, like he'd missed out on something.

Missed out.

Why did that ring a bell in my head?

"You're not the only one who missed out, Rosie."

Buzz and the Eared Grebe he'd spotted yesterday morning!

When we met Buzz on the deck, he told Rosie he'd texted some birders he knew, but then the bird was gone before they arrived. He'd mentioned Cynnie Scott and Birdy . . . was Mark another birder that Buzz had tried to reach?

If so, that would probably explain Mark's roaring into the parking lot. Then, if he'd gotten the text the bird was gone before he even stepped into the park, maybe he'd be so frustrated at missing the rarity, he'd just turn around and leave.

Like he did, leaving his uncle as the only birder to see the Eared Grebe.

If Buzz really did see the grebe . . .

Not that birders were a suspicious bunch as a whole, but the fact was, a lone birder making a sighting of a rarity could seem questionable under the best circumstances. If that birder had a rocky relationship with one of the birders who missed seeing the bird . . .

Would Mark think his uncle lied about seeing the grebe?

Mark accused Buzz of being a liar, and knowing from counseling experience how messy relationships could get when alcoholism was involved, I didn't doubt Mark had a whole list of grievances against his uncle who was trying to help him get help. For all I knew, Mark made it a habit of comparing himself to his uncle, and every time he came up short, it only added fuel to the fire that was eating away at their relationship.

They needed help. Both of them.

But not from me.

I was on vacation, or at least, that had been the plan.

A birding vacation.

Heck, I would have liked to see that Eared Grebe myself. It must have been a prize for Buzz, too, since he said he'd also called Cynnie Scott to come out and see it. That was a smart move, and I believed that it proved Buzz did, indeed, see the grebe, because he wouldn't call a local legend to verify his sighting unless he really had the sighting.

Although . . . every birder knew, too well unfortunately, that birds—especially rarities, it seemed—had minds of their own. Presuming that a particular bird would patiently wait for a second birder to arrive and confirm its identification was downright idiocy; fervently hoping it might wait around, or reappear later, was a much more reasonable approach. Assuring you could get that second confirmation was one of the best reasons to bird with a buddy, if you asked me.

That, and having someone to commiserate with when you'd spent the day trying to track down a reported rarity and ended up instead with another empty tank of gas and a speeding ticket besides.

I mean, I loved our state patrol and our outstate gas stations, but seeing less of both of them wouldn't break my heart.

So the fact that no one joined Buzz in seeing the Eared Grebe could beg the question, then: did Buzz really see the grebe, or was he trying to construct an alibi for himself during the time of Birdy's murder? Once another birder arrived, it would be simple enough to tell him, or her, that the bird had just flown. It happened all the time.

Without another birder to back him up with the bird sighting, Buzz had no alibi.

He did, however, have a really big walking stick that looked like it could inflict some serious damage if you found yourself at the wrong end of it.

Great. I was back to pinning a murder on Birdy's best friend.

On the upside, I may have hit on the explanation for Mark's sudden arrival and departure in the parking lot at Estero Llano on the morning of Birdy's murder. So why did I feel like I was still missing an important clue from Crazy Eddie's recording?

As I waited for the gate to slide open at the Birds Nest to allow me to drive onto the property, a Great Kiskadee landed on one of the bushes near the garage.

It was not the one-eyed individual that seemed to keep turning up where we birded. I wondered if seeing the bird at Quinta Mazatlan had spooked me into considering it an omen, and that was the reason I'd spent much of the day fixated on Mark Myers as a suspect. Normally, I didn't subscribe to superstitions and omens, and even though birds were famous for their associations with those things in folklore and legends, I tried not to judge birds by their literary reputations. I liked to see birds objectively for what they were—amazing creatures that shared my space whenever I was outside.

And that sentiment brought me back to a consideration of the big space topic among the MOBsters: the SpaceX space port location outside Boca Chica Beach. Thanks to the chief, I knew what role Buzz had played in landing the project at Boca Chica, but I was still in the dark when it came to Birdy's involvement. As an avionics engineer, he'd worked at NASA, according to Eddie, and I knew that the drone being tested for finding drug smugglers was his design; why Birdy had been hailed with Buzz in the photo and article about last year's citrus parade was still a mystery.

And whether or not it had anything to do with his death was likewise a big fat question mark for me.

Face it, Bob, I told myself. *You're not going to figure this one out. And as long as you stay out of trouble for another forty-eight hours, you don't have to. Bird with Luce, watch a parade, and let the chief do his job.*

That was probably the best advice I'd given myself in years.

I just hoped I could take it.

Chapter Eighteen

Twelve hours later, Luce and I were both still alive and well, getting ready to cross off the last bird sightings we hoped to make during our trip to the Lower Rio Grande Valley.

After an early dinner on Thursday, we'd gone back to Weslaco to catch the nightly flocking of the Red-Crowned Parrots that Eddie had urged us to see. The birds weren't hard to find. All we did was drive around the older neighborhoods with our windows rolled down, and sure enough, about twenty minutes before sunset, we could hear them coming from blocks away, squawking and calling. We followed the noise, and witnessed close to 125 Red-crowned Parrots coming to roost in the trees lining a residential area. The noise was almost deafening, and I hoped the people who lived there all owned stock in earplugs.

No MOBsters crossed our path in our pursuit of the parrots, and that night was a quiet one at the Birds Nest, with no dog alarms or notes tacked on our guest suite door.

This morning, we were starting the day with our second trip to Bentsen-Rio Grande Valley State Park. Once again, the sun was out, and the air was warm. With the car windows rolled down, a light breeze tickled my face. I could almost forget that back home, Old Man Winter was still dumping inches upon inches of snow in my backyard.

"I have an idea," I said to Luce as we passed by a new housing development just outside Bentsen-Rio Grande. "Let's play 'let's pretend' and go look at some model homes. We can imagine what it would be like to live where you never have ice freezing your back patio door shut three months out of the year."

Luce laughed. "That's true. Just think! We could spend all our time birding right here, right where the two migratory corridors—the Central and the Mississippi—"

"Converge," we said in unison.

"You could give senior birding tours," she reminded me. "CPR included. I bet you'd be a huge hit, especially with all the ladies."

I watched the last house of the row of model homes disappear from my rear view mirror.

"On second thought," I said, "frozen doors aren't that bad, especially when I have a gorgeous wife cooking something good and hot in the oven."

Luce laughed again. "You are such a chauvinist."

"No, I'm not," I protested. "I'm practical. You're a chef, I'm not. It just happens that you're also gorgeous. I'm simply making an observation. That's what I do. I observe. Birds. Students. My wife. I'm a master of detail."

This time, Luce snickered. "Okay, master of detail. What is today's date?"

I drew a blank.

"No fair," I said. "We're on vacation. I don't keep track of dates when we're on vacation."

"Then you're not a master of detail, Bobby," she chided me. "If you were, you'd know why today's date is important."

Oh, no.

I frantically searched my memory for anything that would tip me off to why today's date was important, but nothing surfaced.

It wasn't Luce's birthday.

It wasn't our wedding anniversary.

I was positive that Valentine's Day was next month.

Crap.

It was one of *those* moments—the ones that fill the heart of every married man with dread: I'd forgotten something important, or at least, something that was important to my wife.

Note that the two are not always the same: something important, and something important to my wife.

Never, however, will a man say that to his lovely bride.

Unless he's looking for a night or two out on the sofa instead of in his own bed.

What was the big deal about the date?

"You don't know, do you?" Luce asked.

I could have sworn she sounded amused. Of course, she knew I didn't know. My wife can always read my mind, even when I can't.

I slowly shook my head, my eyes focused on the left-hand turn lane ahead that would take us into the state park.

"I am a failure as a husband," I admitted.

My wife laughed once more.

"Oh, no, you're not," she assured me. "You're just not good with numbers, Mr. Master of Details."

"I know how many more Valley specialties we need to find," I defended myself, making my left turn towards Bentsen-Rio Grande, "to make this trip a perfect grand slam."

"Oh, I think this trip has been perfect even if we don't find the last few specialties," she said. "Aside from a murder, Eddie getting framed, and our threatening note, that is."

She placed her left hand over my right on the steering wheel and gave it a warm, soft squeeze. "This trip is a life-changing experience, if you ask me."

I nodded in agreement. "The kind of birding you can do around here is nothing short of amazing, that's for sure. It's set a whole new bar for birding trips, as far as I'm concerned."

Beside me, Luce laughed.

"You got that right," she said.

I parked the car in the half-full lot, and we walked along the sidewalk into the main entrance of Bentsen-Rio Grande. I scanned the tops of the trees that lined the road, and caught the profile of an approaching bird.

"Some kind of hawk," I said, lifting my binoculars.

It flew directly overhead, giving me a clear look at its broad wings, gray body, and the three wide bands of black feathers on its tail.

"My, my," Luce said, her voice holding a hint of awe. "A Gray Hawk. Now that's a bird you don't see every day."

"Not even around here," I replied, feeling my own excitement kicking in at the unexpected sighting. "It's a permanent resident, but I guess the locals don't see it frequently."

Why that was the case, I wasn't sure. A member of the southern buteo family, the Gray Hawk is mostly found south of the Mexican border. Yet on all the bird lists we'd seen at the World Birding Centers, the Gray Hawk was considered uncommon for the area, so to have one fly right over our heads was a real score with which to start our last full day of birding along the Rio Grande.

"Good thing the birds don't have to have papers to cross into the U.S.," I commented. "I'd hate to see what immigration laws would do to our life lists if that were the case."

From behind me, I heard the sound of wheels rolling and squeaking. I turned around and watched a young couple pulling along a canoe on wheels. Fishing poles stuck out on one side of the craft.

"Fishing on the Rio Grande today?" I called to the two.

The fellow nodded. "There's a good spot to put in at the edge of the park," he called back. "As long as we don't drift over the international border, we're fine."

Apparently, fish didn't need papers either to cross the border, although they did run the risk of getting eaten if they got caught.

As far as I knew, the human type of illegal immigrants just got sent back to Mexico.

We watched the couple head off on one of the roads inside the park, towing their canoe behind them.

"I wish we could use wheels when we transport our canoe in the Boundary Waters instead of portaging it on our heads," Luce observed. "I'd be inclined to stay in the wilderness and enjoy it a lot more if I didn't have to carry around a canoe."

A vision of the canoe lying atop Birdy Johnson at Alligator Lake popped into my head.

Why was a canoe on Alligator Lake? There were, after all, alligators in Alligator Lake. I assumed that a body of water frequented by big reptiles with very sharp teeth and surprising speed would not be a popular spot for watersports.

Had Birdy used the canoe to go place his sensors? I knew from looking at maps of the park that a trail around the lake led to the shore where Birdy's body was found, and I'd guessed that was how he'd gotten there. But if that were the case, how did the canoe get there?

I looked in the direction the young couple with the canoe had gone, and it occurred to me that perhaps Birdy's killer had used the canoe to approach Birdy as quietly as possible so as to catch him unaware. Canoes on wheels might make a lot of noise, but a canoe in the water was virtually silent. Paddling the canoe across the lake would also be a quicker way to reach Birdy than taking the trail that wound around the lake. And if the killer heard others approaching on the opposite shore, it would be a simple matter to escape the scene of the murder by slipping into the woods behind it.

None of which gave me a clue as to who might have guided that canoe across the water to kill Birdy. It did, however, tell me that Birdy's murder was well planned out ahead of time. His killer knew exactly how to get away with murder.

A MOB hitman?

For some reason, I seriously doubted that a birding club of senior citizens required the services of a professional killer. What would be the reason? To keep birders in line if they made false reports of rarities?

Surely a slap on the wrist would be sufficient. Heck, a simple email rejection did the trick for us in Minnesota. Besides, it wasn't like the MOB was a secret enclave of world-class competitive birders vying for international birding stardom.

After the few days I'd spent around the MOBsters, I'd gotten the impression that a lot of them were happy just to be able to get out and about and see whatever happened to be flying by. Their attitude reminded me of every birder I've ever met: birding was fun. Unlike some hobbies that required peak physical conditioning or over-the-top stamina, birding offered enjoyment for whatever level of activity an individual might choose. I knew a lot of birders, for example, who found their favorite birdwatching right in their own backyards, usually equipped with a multitude of stocked bird feeders for their feathered visitors and comfortable lounge chairs for themselves. I also knew birders who'd traveled the world to see exotic rarities. It didn't matter if you were new at it or had years of experience, birding was a hobby anyone could enjoy regardless of age, financial situation, health conditions, or skill.

Birds were everywhere.

At that very moment, my own "everywhere" was a rustic feeding station just outside the exhibit center of the Bentsen-Rio Grande Valley State Park. A noisy flock of more than thirty Plain Chachalacas mobbed the dirt floor of the cleared area that hosted a variety of bird feeders. When we'd visited here earlier in the week, we'd watched park staffers refilling feeders in different locations around the park and marveled at the way the birds seemed to time their arrivals to coincide with the refilling of the feeders.

I don't know if birds can tell time, but they sure knew when it was time to eat and where.

On second thought, maybe it wasn't any different than the way I showed up in our kitchen every night just before Luce started making dinner.

Yes, it was true: a Bob White could be trained.

As the last of the rowdy avian crowd on the ground dispersed, a Green Jay flew through the clearing to land on a feeding platform strewn with seeds. Three more of the birds immediately joined the first one, each of them repeatedly dipping their brilliant blue heads to pick up seeds. Their jet-black bibs reached up and over their eyes, while their mostly green bodies blended in with the greenery behind them. Meanwhile, in a tree nearby, a Great Kiskadee loudly announced its own arrival at the feeding station with a triple riff of its signature bird call.

"It's Grand Central Station around here," Luce commented.

"Rio Grande Central Station," I corrected her.

"Hey, Bob!"

Luce and I both turned in the direction of the human call to see Cynnie Scott making her way over to us from the exhibit center. Dressed in faded blue jeans and a rolled-sleeve work shirt, the local birding legend had a pair of binoculars around her neck and a set of keys in her hand. Today her long silver hair was tied back into a fat ponytail.

"I just got a text from some birders down by the river," she said, "they say they're looking at that Eared Grebe I missed two days ago at Estero Llano. Want to join me?"

She held up the keys and jingled them. "I'm borrowing a park cart to get over there pronto," she explained. "I'm not missing it again!"

"We'd love to," I said. I grabbed Luce's hand and we followed Cynnie to an enclosure behind the feeding station where a cart was parked. A huge sack of seed took up the space behind the cramped second row of seats in the cart, so I directed Luce into the passenger seat next to Cynnie and climbed into the back row myself. The naturalist fired up the cart and whipped the little vehicle around to head towards the park trail down to the Rio Grande's shore.

"I'm sorry we didn't get to visit more the other night at Buzz's," Cynnie said. "The club always prides itself on having one of the best floats in the Citrus Parade, and I'm afraid we fell behind schedule this year with our planning and building."

She raised an arm to point upwards at a long pouch hanging from a tree off the side of the road.

"That's an Altamira Oriole's nest," she said.

It was almost two feet long, I guessed, woven of roots and branches and suspended neatly from the tree's branch.

"I've seen the birds hunting for smashed grasshoppers on the fronts of cars," Cynnie tossed out as she zipped along in the park's converted golf cart. "I don't know if that means Altamira Orioles are lazy or opportunistic. There they are!"

This time, she pointed at two of the bright orange and black birds as they foraged along tree branches on the opposite side of the road from the nest we'd seen. The Altamira Oriole also sported a black bib, though its bib narrowed below its beak unlike the broader one of the Green Jay.

"I also felt I owed you an apology for sounding so negative about SpaceX," the MOB president added as we bounced along in the little cart. "It's going to be a boon for the local economy and provide a lot of jobs, which is a good thing for this area. I just get so disappointed that we have to keep trading off conservation for economic growth."

"It happens everywhere," I said. "The upside is when it motivates people to be more conscientious about what we can do to preserve what we still have. Like 3M using their technology to develop bird-safe glass," I reminded her.

Cynnie nodded as she pulled into a gravel space near the trail that led down to the river.

"That's true," she agreed. She turned off the cart and we all got out. "Come this way."

She led us on a short path that opened up to the Rio Grande.

"And sometimes, good birding karma just happens," Cynnie said to us over her shoulder. "I heard a rumor last night that a start-up conservation group is making a bid for some land north of the SpaceX site to establish a new preserve. If they can get it, that might just provide the habitat our displaced birds are going to need when SpaceX is up and running."

"Has that been hard for the MOB?" Luce asked. "I mean, you're the president and one of your members sold the land to the spaceport developer."

I glanced at Luce, who was trotting along with me after Cynnie. She lifted her hands in a "well, I thought I'd ask" gesture.

"Oh, sure, I was mad at Buzz for a while," Cynnie admitted, "as were several of the club members, but Rosalie and Birdy were always defending Buzz's decision to everyone. They said he had a plan he was working on. They said he was a sharpshooter, and not just because he used to win medals for it when he was in the service. Buzz was smart, Birdy said, and he always did the right thing, even when it hurt."

The word "sharpshooter" stuck in my gut, and I thought of Eddie crouching beside my car with a bullet graze bleeding on his calf.

Buzz Davis was a sharpshooter.

Before I could explore that idea, however, Cynnie turned around for a moment to look me in the eye.

"You know that Buzz resigned from the astronaut program to enter rehab, don't you?"

"Yes," I said.

"He resigned?" Luce asked. "He didn't get kicked out when Birdy reported him?"

"Birdy never reported anything that Buzz didn't want him to," Cynnie said. "Birdy knew that Buzz was in trouble with alcohol, but he didn't turn him in to their superiors, if that's what you're thinking. The truth is that Birdy helped Buzz get himself into a treatment program. But the guys knew there would be an investigation about Buzz's performance prior to his resignation, and if it had become known that Birdy knew about Buzz's addiction, Birdy would have been in trouble for not reporting Buzz as soon as he was aware of the alcohol problem."

"So Buzz protected Birdy by having Birdy publicly blow the whistle on him," I finished for her. "Buzz didn't want Birdy's career crashed with his own."

"That's right," Cynnie said. "Those two guys were best friends their whole lives. As far as I know, the only thing that ever came between them was a 'who,' not a thing."

"Rosalie," Luce said. "They were both in love with Rosalie."

Chapter Nineteen

Cynnie smiled at Luce. "You can see it, can't you? The three of them have been good friends for decades, but Buzz has been in love with her for years. Of course, she was married for many of those years, so Buzz never shared his feelings with her. Then, when Rosalie's husband died five years ago, she and Birdy became really close, probably because Birdy had lost his wife years before that. I've heard that sharing that kind of grieving experience can be very bonding for people."

"So Buzz lost his chance," I concluded.

I shook my head in disbelief. On top of everything else, there was a love triangle involving Birdy Johnson. And Buzz Davis, who happened to be an eagle eye with a rifle, had a plan he was keeping secret from the MOB.

Geez Louise. Let a Hollywood scriptwriter get a hold of this murder, and it was going to be a miniseries that ran for years.

"I hope that Eared Grebe is still here," I finally said, "because my crime-solving karma just bottomed out."

"Stop right there!" a voice commanded us. "On the ground. Now!"

The three of us turned to our left, where the voice had come from. A uniformed man stepped out from behind a thicket of mesquite. He had a gun on his hip and a nametag on his jacket.

"I said to get down on the ground!"

Cynnie propped her hands on her hips and yelled back, "Ricky, for crying out loud, you know me!"

I glanced from the slowly advancing man to Cynnie.

"You sure?" I asked her. I was ready to drop if the man's hand wandered anywhere near the gun. I'd have to tackle Luce down with me and cover her body with my own.

I know, I'm an old-fashioned kind of guy with an outdated perspective on women.

So sue me.

But I'm still protecting my wife.

"Yes," Cynnie said, rolling her eyes, making me feel marginally relieved. "He's Border Patrol. He stops me about once a week when I bird near the river. I'm not hitting the ground, Ricky!" she shouted at him.

"Oh, come on, Cynnie," Ricky responded as he approached. "It's a slow day. Give me something to do." He stopped a few feet away and nodded at me and Luce. "Birding with Cynnie, right?"

"Yes," Luce told him, holding her hands up at shoulder level in mock surrender. "You caught us red-handed, I'm afraid."

"This is Bob White. His wife, Luce," Cynnie introduced us to the officer. "They're here from Minnesota."

"Lucy?" The man's face lit up. "I'm Ricky! Ricky Ricardo! 'Lucy, I'm home!'" he said, doing a pretty decent imitation of Desi Arnaz from the classic *I Love Lucy* television series. "I grew up watching that show," he enthused. "My mom loved Lucille Ball, and she had all those shows on tapes. You'd have to get them on DVDs now."

I checked out his name tag.

It really was Ricardo.

"It's Luce," my wife corrected him. "But I watched all those shows, too. I loved the chocolate factory episode."

"What are you doing here, Ricky?" Cynnie asked. "I usually see you on the other side of the park."

Ricky propped his own hands on his hips.

"We had a tip there might be an attempted river crossing sometime today," he told us. "If it's a boatload of mothers and children, like it usually has been lately, we want to be sure they get turned over to the right authorities. So far, nothing's going on," he finished. "Except for a couple birders who walked by here about ten minutes ago."

"That's who we're looking for," Cynnie said. "They spotted a rarity."

"Have at it," Ricky said. He gave us a short salute and went back into the thicket.

"He stops you once a week?" I asked Cynnie as we headed towards the shoreline.

"Yes," she answered. "Because I know the area so well, and I've been birding here for so long, I tend to sometimes go where I want when I probably shouldn't."

"Meaning?" Luce asked.

"Meaning this is a sensitive area and issue for the Border Patrol because of drug, weapons, or human smuggling, and I don't always put their concerns ahead of mine when I'm looking for a bird. Which is probably pretty dumb," she added, "since the patrol just wants to keep everyone safe and secure, including the illegals who cross the border. I've never been arrested, though, so I keep going where I want."

I suddenly recalled a story I'd heard years ago from a birder I know. At the time, I thought he was exaggerating, but now, I had no doubt Joe had been telling me the truth. He'd gone to bird around Falcon Dam, which is farther north along the Rio Grande, on the Texas side. After a full day at the dam, Joe got in the car to leave, only to find that the battery was dead. By then, it was dark. Out of nowhere, several heavily armed border guards dressed in dark combat uniforms appeared in the parking lot and confronted Joe. Fortunately for my friend, the guards accepted his birding story (I'm sure the binoculars and birding guides in the car helped) and didn't arrest him for smuggling. They did help him restart his car, however, and sent him on his way.

It made me very glad that we'd run into Ricky Ricardo during full daylight.

Besides, I really didn't want to add an arrest in Texas to my permanent record. A multitude of Minnesota speeding tickets, I could manage. Getting booked and a mug shot in Texas would be another story.

A story I'd rather not have to explain to my boss back at Savage High School.

Being a murder suspect in the past has been bad enough, but having to explain being mistaken for a drug smuggler might be even worse.

Can you say "goodbye state pension"?

We turned a bend along the shore and spotted a trio of birders Cynnie recognized. They all had binoculars up.

I followed the direction of their sight lines into the river and put my own binos to my eyes.

An Eared Grebe.

"Yes!" Cynnie said as she studied the bird in her sights. "And I've got confirmation with other birders. Take that, Buzz Davis!"

Luce murmured something, and I lowered my binoculars to see what she was doing.

"Over there," she said, pointing to a log that was pinned against the shore of the Rio Grande on the American side of the border. It was a marshy area, almost tucked back out of sight from where we stood. I could see two long-legged birds perched on the log.

"Baby White Ibis," Luce said.

I focused on the birds. They were cleaning their feathers and soaking up the warm Texas sunshine, their long bills slivers of light. Framed by the river and the shore, the birds were the picture of tranquility. Watching them, it was hard to imagine that the same river was the setting for the border conflicts that humans continued to wage.

"It's beautiful, isn't it?" Cynnie commented.

Yes, yet another woman could read my thoughts. Sometimes I wondered why I even bothered to speak out loud.

"It's hard to reconcile all this natural beauty with the nasty human complications around here," Luce responded.

See what I mean? My mind is an open book for women, apparently.

"You know, I've lived here my whole life," Cynnie continued. "Growing up, my family went back and forth across the border with ease. We loved going to Reynosa for shopping and the food. No one ever worried about safety."

I took a final look at the ibis youngsters. Ignorance can be bliss . . . but it can also get you arrested on the Rio Grande if you land on the wrong shore.

"Hey, you guys!" Cynnie called to the birders further up the shore. "Thanks for the text. We saw the grebe. Did you see the two ibis?"

"We did," one of the trio shouted back, waving a farewell to us. "Good birding!"

The threesome walked off onto a wooded trail, leaving us alone on the shore of the Rio Grande. Cynnie turned around and led us back to where we'd left the park cart.

"Of course, when I was a kid," Cynnie resumed her reminiscing as we climbed back into the cart, "there were a lot more farm fields and citrus orchards around. A lot of them have become housing areas now as the cities have grown. I miss all the cotton fields, but you should see the sorghum fields after they're harvested—the farmers burn the fields, and it's an excellent time to watch for raptors hunting the exposed rodents. When the fields are burning, you can see flakes of burned plants floating down like black snow in neighborhoods even miles away."

I tried to imagine what black snow would look like and decided it would make a long winter even bleaker.

"I'll stick with the white kind we get at home," I told our impromptu birding guide. "It may be cold, but at least it's bright when the sun comes out. Black yards sound really depressing."

Cynnie laughed. "Yes, I guess it is kind of ghoulish. It sure makes it easy to spot white birds, though."

She pulled into the gravel area where we'd found the park cart. "You guys done here for the morning?"

"Let's see—a Gray Hawk, Plain Chachalacas, Green Jays, Great Kiskadee, Altamira Oriole, Eared Grebe, and White Ibis," I listed. "*No esta* bad, as Rosalie would say. Yeah, I think we're done."

As I helped Luce climb out of the cart's front passenger seat, Cynnie caught my eye for a final word.

"I'd appreciate it if you didn't say anything to Buzz about what I told you regarding his feelings for Rosalie," she said. "He's got more than enough on his plate right now with Birdy's murder."

"Who said it was murder?" I asked her. Hadn't Chief Pacheco said his people were keeping that information from the public?

Cynnie looked at me in surprise. "Of course it's a murder case. There was a canoe turned over Birdy to hide his body. People who die of natural causes don't pull a canoe over themselves before they gasp their last breath."

"Good conclusion," I conceded. "So, who do you think killed Birdy Johnson?"

"I don't know, and I'm not sure I want to find out," Cynnie said.

"Why do you say that?" Luce asked her.

"Because I'm afraid it might be someone associated with the MOB," she confided, "and I know these people. At least, I thought I did. The idea that someone you know could be someone else entirely is very disturbing, not to mention frightening. It makes you wonder how much of what you think is a lie."

"Why do you think it's a MOBster?" I asked her.

"What?" Cynnie looked confused.

"A MOBster—one of the MOB members," I clarified for her. "Why are you suspicious of your club members?"

Cynnie blew out a breath of air. "Because they all knew Birdy. Isn't that the conventional wisdom—that murder victims are typically killed by someone they know? Well, we've got a whole flock of birders with personal connections to Birdy, so I suspect Chief Pacheco is at this very moment sifting through everything he can find out about every one of the MOB members. Including me."

I had a very strong hunch the most important part of that little speech was the very last word out of Cynnie's mouth: me.

I put my hands on the side of the cart and leaned toward the woman. "What are you really afraid of, Cynnie?"

She gave me a look that was part defiance and part resignation.

"I'm afraid Chief Pacheco is going to arrest me for Birdy's murder, because at a public hearing last month about SpaceX, I told Birdy he'd better watch his back if he continued to support the sale of Buzz's land for the project."

"You threatened him? Publicly?"

Cynnie shut her eyes and laid her forehead on the cart's steering wheel.

"Yes," she confessed. "I was furious with Birdy. I couldn't understand how he could support a project that was going to do so much damage to our bird populations. It was probably the stupidest thing I've ever done."

She lightly banged her head on the wheel. Her silver ponytail bounced on her back.

"Make that the second most stupid thing I've ever done," she said into the wheel.

"I'm afraid to ask," I said, "but what did you do that was worse than making a public threat against Birdy Johnson?"

A strangled laugh came up from the wheel.

"I fell in love with Buzz Davis."

Chapter Twenty

"Why can't any of these people control themselves?" I asked Luce as we walked back to the Birds Nest after getting lunch at a nearby *taqueria*.

Knowing that it was our last full day in McAllen, we'd decided to walk the few blocks to the small taco shop in order to soak up as much sun and warmth as we could before we had to head home to Minnesota's cold tomorrow. We had chosen wisely, too, since the handmade chicken tacos, homemade tortilla chips and salsa bar had been so amazingly good that lunch had totally driven all thoughts of MOBsters from my mind while we'd feasted.

Now, though, the crazy web of relationships and possible motives behind Birdy's murder had regained its spotlight in my head. Not for the first time, I mentally cursed my counseling instinct to set things right, which seemed, more often than not, just to make matters worse.

"Because they're normal human beings?" Luce suggested, looping her hand around my arm.

"I'm beginning to doubt that," I said. "I'm to the point where I actually think I'm going to wake up any minute now and say, 'wow—it was all a dream.'"

Luce patted my arm and yawned. "Speaking of dreamtime, I really need to lie down for a while this afternoon. Do you mind?"

I kissed her cheek. "Of course not. You sleep, and I'll sit out on the back porch and envy Rhonda for all the birds that come to her feeders. I'm pretty sure we're not going to be seeing any Great Kiskadees or Golden-fronted Woodpeckers in our yard when we get back."

After an hour of watching the parade of Texas birds that frequented Rhonda's urban bird heaven, I was nodding off myself, lulled into total relaxation in the hammock strung up on the edge of the porch. I almost didn't hear my cell phone's distinctive chirping ring tone through my post-lunch siesta. By the time I fumbled it out of my pocket, I'd missed the call. A quick check at the phone's log told me that it had been Eddie.

I called him back.

"You're still with us," I said. "Good. Nobody shooting at you today, huh?"

Eddie's voice boomed through the phone. "Nope. Just me and my bodyguard buddy, who still hasn't developed a sense of humor. I think everyone else has forgotten I exist, except for the chief," he said. "Pacheco was here this morning to tell me the investigation into Birdy's death and my shooting has stalled out. No new leads and no evidence."

If that were the case, Cynnie Scott didn't have anything to worry about. I was certain that, if Pacheco could turn up any reason to question her further, he would have done so by now. I thought briefly of trying to call Cynnie to let her off the hook of her fear of arrest, but I didn't have her contact information. What would I say, anyway?

Hey, Cynnie—that second most stupid thing you've ever done? Not to worry. Chief Pacheco knows it was just a stupid thing and not a reason to arrest you. But about that most stupid thing? Sorry, can't help you there.

"Pacheco says he's totally stumped," Eddie continued over the phone. "He even ran background checks on all the MOB, hoping something interesting might pop up, but he came up with nothing. He said he's beginning to think it might be a random shooting after all."

"Except for your bottle of Aquavit showing up near Birdy's body," I reminded him. "That can't be random."

"You wouldn't think so, would you?" Eddie agreed with me. "I still think someone tried to frame me, but who knows? Maybe whoever picked it up when I lost it helping with the float was meaning to return it to me, but they lost it while birding."

"In the same vicinity as where Birdy was killed?" I asked. "I don't think so, Eddie."

"Well, Bob, if you have any miraculous revelations about who killed Birdy, and why, I'm sure Chief Pacheco would be happy to hear about it," Eddie said. "Judging from his comments, I think the chief is about ready to throw in the towel on this one."

We talked a few more minutes about his progress on the drone, and I told him Luce and I were going to be leaving for home after tomorrow's Citrus Festival Parade. I went back to dozing in the hammock, but not before I turned my cell phone off.

What's good for the goose is good for the gander, I decided.

Hello, naptime.

And just before I fell asleep, I finally knew what it was that had struck me about Eddie's recording at the Estero Llano parking lot. Aside from Birdy, Poppy Mac was the only one with a knapsack. Buzz had carried his impressive walking stick, binoculars tucked in a case attached to his belt, and Gunnar, Schooner, and Paddy had binoculars hanging on their chests.

Their Hawaiian shirt-covered chests.

But unless they had interior pockets on those shirts, none of the MOB magpies were bringing along a bottle of Aquavit.

Paddy's wife, though . . . she could easily have a small liquor bottle stashed in that bag.

Heck, she could have had a hammer in there for all I knew.

It occurred to me then that Buzz had had a backpack when we'd first encountered him on the deck on Wednesday morning. I wondered where he had picked it up, since Crazy Eddie's recording plainly showed him backpack-less when he'd arrived. Had there been some kind of hand-off in the park?

I had a bad feeling that if a hand-off was happening in Estero Llano early in the morning in secluded areas, it probably wasn't a cookie exchange.

When Poppy had mentioned the other day that the area had long been known for drug smuggling and illegal immigration, I'd passed it off as a local reputation that might or might not be accurate, sort of like how almost every college in America says it's the biggest party school in the nation. After our own encounter with Border Patrol at Bentsen-Rio Grande, though, I had personal proof that illegal activity along the Mexican-American border was a fact of life.

Crap.

I'd already crossed Buzz Davis off my suspect list, and now I was going to have to put him back on, because I didn't know where he'd gotten a backpack, or what was in it. On top of that, when I added what I'd learned that morning about the former astronaut's sharpshooting ability along with his unrequited love for Rosalie, I figured I'd better promote the man to the number one suspect position. Why Buzz might want to hurt Eddie was beyond me, but the man clearly had the skills to do it. As for motive to kill his best friend, long-simmering resentment and revenge could rank right up there with passionate competition.

Gee, whoever thinks that age can slow a man down could learn a thing or two from Buzz Davis.

I wasn't sure if they would necessarily be good things to learn, however.

And then I realized I had a question for Chief Pacheco that might finally help him get closer to identifying Birdy's killer.

What, exactly, cracked open Birdy's head? Was it the impact of a fall, or the impact of a weapon?

If the former, then I had nothing to offer Pacheco. If it was the latter, I knew two people who could have been carrying a concealed weapon in Estero Llano on the morning that Birdy Johnson was killed: Poppy Mac and Buzz Davis.

Definitely not two of a kind. Aside from their mutual interest in birds, Poppy and Mac seemed as unalike as a . . . Plain Chachalaca and a Zone-tailed Hawk.

Which, by the way, I'd hoped we might see ever since Schooner had mentioned it the other day. It would be a lifer for both Luce and me.

Another lifer, I should say. We'd already added more lifers to our list during this trip than we'd found in the last three years back home in Minnesota. I guessed I was just being greedy.

And human, right?

Doesn't everyone want to go for all the gusto they can get?

Luce and I had jumped at an unexpected opportunity to visit the Lower Rio Grande Valley, and here we were, enjoying sunshine and birding in January.

Lots of the MOBsters had decided to retire here and enjoy the climate and birding year-round.

Buzz Davis had sold the family land and apparently made a fortune.

Poppy Mac wanted to ride on the first spaceship to launch from SpaceX.

Gusto. Life. Live it.

I sounded like a beer commercial.

I called Eddie back and asked him to show the chief the recording again. I explained what I'd been considering, and he agreed it was worth another look, and that he'd get right on it and call the chief. Luce woke up, we had an early dinner at Roosevelt's in McAllen, then went out to the corner of Tenth and Trenton streets to watch the nightly performance that Rhonda, our Birds Nest hostess, had recommended we see: the amassing of the blackbirds along the telephone wires.

Seriously, it was like a scene from that classic Hitchcock thriller "The Birds," but longer in duration and in physical area. I parked the car in the Target store lot, and Luce and I got out to lean against the hood of the SUV. Four of the eight overhead wires were already crowded with blackbirds, who constantly shifted and hopped aside to allow room for more incoming birds. Gradually as the sun lowered in the sky and the night fell, the noise level of the gathering birds increased, until I had to raise my voice to speak with Luce beside me.

"This is creepy," I said, staring at what must have been thousands of blackbirds perched on the wires that ran in all directions. Silhouetted by the fading light, the birds seemed to grow in size and numbers, until the whole intersection was a study in black and white—black birds, black utility poles, white car lights and the white faces of people passing by in cars. It reminded me of an old black-and-white movie with sinister characters and gangland shootouts.

Which got me thinking about the local MOB.

They weren't exactly sinister with their Hawaiian shirts, floppy hats, hearing aids and binoculars.

But because of Eddie's bottle of Aquavit and the fact that all the birders knew where Birdy would be on an early Wednesday morning, I was more convinced than ever that one of them had killed Birdy.

And tried to shoot Eddie.

And with that thought, I finally hit on why someone would target those two particular men and want me and Luce to get out of the area: the drone.

Birdy asked Crazy Eddie to help him with the project. Eddie had joined the MOB when he arrived, and like any close-knit flock, the MOBsters all knew each other's business, or at the least, *thought* they knew each other's business. As Eddie had pointed out, some folks, like Rosalie, thought the drone project was all about immigration control, while others believed it was for cracking down on drug smuggling.

If I had to pick which group might be more dangerous to tangle with over Eddie and Birdy's drone work, I would guess drug dealers. Based on everything I'd ever read or heard about the illicit drug trade, I assumed huge amounts of money were involved, and the people running the smuggling rings weren't always nice about it, to say the least. Think violence, shoot-outs, murder, gore and revenge. True, I didn't know that for a fact, but I hoped I never had the occasion to, either.

Nor did I have any personal experience with illegal immigrants, other than a few students who seemed to have slipped through the cracks of bureaucracy and ended up enrolled in our high school. The business of bringing in undocumented foreign-born individuals for profit was so far out of my worldview I couldn't begin to grasp all the technicalities and legislation surrounding its prosecution; from a simple comparison of profit versus risk, it seemed like the drug dealers had more to lose from discovery by drones.

Ergo, my choice of drug runners as the bad guys who were after Birdy and Eddie.

As for our threatening note, I figured that was damage control of some kind because we were personal friends of Crazy Eddie's. Maybe whoever was behind the attack on Eddie was warning us away so he, or she, wouldn't have to add us to the target list.

A considerate killer?

That was an oxymoron, wasn't it? Killers were supposed to be heartless, not kind. I seriously doubted that, in the annals of murderers, there was a page devoted to killers most likely to be named "Mr. or Ms. Congeniality." For some reason, I just couldn't picture a bunch of murderers hanging out together to confer titles on each other, like a bunch of student editors getting together to name classmates as "Best Athlete" or "Most Likely to Succeed" for the school yearbook. That would take a consensus, and . . .

Oh. My. Gosh.

A terrible possibility slipped into my head.

What if the entire MOB was involved in Birdy's death?

What if the MOB was, in truth, a *real* mob dealing drugs, and Birdy had caught them in the act?

Holy crap.

Chapter Twenty-One

Even though we had another quiet night at the Birds Nest, I didn't sleep very well. I needed to talk to Crazy Eddie and the chief and bounce my new theory off of them. I realized I had no concrete evidence to support any of my speculations, but I was sure I was onto the right track.

My gut, you know. It talks, and I listen.

And sometimes it's even right.

"Bobby," Luce said when I told her of my new set of suspicions over our breakfast of Rhonda's home-made granola and yogurt parfaits, "not that I want to discredit your ability to help the police solve crimes, but seriously, if everyone in the MOB is involved, there is no way Chief Pacheco could have missed a drug ring like that right under his nose. He knows all these people. His mother is one of them."

I gave Luce a noncommittal shrug. "So? Maybe he's in on it."

My wife laid her spoon next to her empty dish and leaned forward, her elbows on the little bistro table. "Do you hear yourself? You sound like a conspiracy theorist. A conspiracy theorist gone nuts, if you want to know the truth."

"But that's just it," I countered. "I do want to know the truth. And I want to know it today," I added.

"Can you handle the truth?" she asked me, a smile starting, then growing, to light up her face. She caught my eyes with hers in a steady gaze.

"I'm pregnant," she announced.

Chapter Twenty-Two

I was really proud of myself. I didn't faint, I didn't jump up and down in a pure adrenaline rush, I didn't roll my eyes, or anything.

Anything.

That's what I didn't do. I didn't, couldn't, do anything for a few moments. I just stared into Luce's brilliant blue eyes, feeling my own face stretch into the biggest smile I'd ever had. Then, without a word, I got out of my chair, and knelt beside my wife's knee, my hand sliding gingerly onto her belly.

"That is the best truth I have ever heard," I said, feeling a dampness rising in my eyes. "Marry me, Luce."

"I already did," she reminded me.

"That's a good thing," I said, wondering why I couldn't seem to come up with something more memorable or romantic or . . . anything.

"My brain has stopped working," I told my wife, who was beginning to laugh at me.

I threw my arms around her and pulled her into me for a long, happy, delirious kiss. When I let her go again, I rocked back on my heels.

"Okay, I think my brain is working again now. I obviously needed oxygen. Thanks for the mouth-to-mouth," I said. I snapped my fingers as I suddenly realized why Luce had been teasing me about dates yesterday morning.

"The date—you missed your monthly cycle," I said, then couldn't help adding, "Mama Luce."

"Happy Valentine's Day, early," she said, her eyes sparkling with mischief. "You know what I feel like doing right now?"

I eyed the door that led back to our bedroom.

Luce gave me a light swat on my chest.

"Wrong," she said, laughing again. "I feel like a parade, and if we get going right now, we can stop in and offer that last minute help the MOB needs to make their Citrus Festival Parade float the very best it has ever been."

I stood and looked down at my wife. "Are you sure? I mean . . ."

I nodded at her midsection.

"I'm pregnant, Bobby, not terminal," she clarified. "And there's nothing like a parade to celebrate good news. Besides, as you yourself pointed out to the chief, the queen herself expects us to be there, and we don't want to keep the queen in suspense."

Fifteen minutes later, I parked the car at one end of Buzz Davis's long driveway behind a line of other vehicles. The MOB float had been moved out of the garage onto the brick-paved apron and to my surprise, the float looked pretty darn good. The front truck cab was clearly now the head of an enormous Green Jay, composed of spray-painted blue oranges, and the trailer behind it sported a citrus-studded map of Texas, along with a collection of a dozen six-foot tall photos featuring the Texas specialty birds. Clumps of people filled the apron around the truck, tacking up last minute grapefruit halves, talking with each other, drinking coffee, and in general, having a grand old time. Behind the float, I spotted a human-sized Great Kiskadee getting a pirate-style black eye patch fitted to his head by none other than the lovely, tiara-crowned Citrus Festival queen herself, Pearl Garcia.

"Look," I said to Luce, pointing at the resplendent Pearl and the costumed birder. "The One-eyed Kiskadee is here. He'll be a local legend by the end of the parade, if he isn't already."

"And there's Mark's Mustang," my wife said, yearning in her voice, pointing at the classic car parked near the float. The Mustang's convertible top was down and the white leather interior gleamed in the early morning sun. "I wonder if it's going to be Pearl's ride during the parade?"

"Yo, Minnesota!"

Schooner waved us over to where he stood near the truck cab door with Chief Pacheco.

"I thought maybe you'd left us and headed home already," he said when we got closer to him.

The words of our midnight warning rang in my head. I threw a quick glance at the chief, but he seemed preoccupied, his gaze directed at his niece Pearl with the giant kiskadee. Could Schooner have been our intruder?

As usual, he was wearing the local birding uniform—a floral print shirt topping a pair of khaki shorts. I almost asked him to turn around for me so I could inspect the shirt for rips, but I couldn't come up with a good line. *Hey, Schooner, I want to check you out* just didn't hit the right note for me.

"We had to see the finished product," I told Schooner, patting the cheek of the truck cab-turned-Green Jay. My hand came away with a tinge of blue on my palm. Okay, so that was one thing I'd gotten right about the MOB: spray-painting grapefruit was an inside job.

"We're leaving after the parade," Luce told him. "We're missing the Winter Carnival parade back home, but I have a feeling this one, in seventy-degree weather, will more than make up for it. It was nice meeting you, Schooner."

With that remark, Luce took my arm and steered me towards the back of the float. Pearl and the kiskadee were nowhere in sight, but Cynnie Scott,MOB president/conservation advocate/unlucky-in-love local legend, reached out to snag my sleeve and draw me into a conversation she was having with Poppy Mac.

"Bob," she said, excitement practically oozing out of her, "and Luce, you two have got to hear this. Buzz just told me he's using the proceeds from his sale of the land to the SpaceX project to fund a new initiative for conservation of key migratory areas! Isn't that fabulous? He's the conservation start-up I mentioned to you yesterday!"

"I knew he was one of the good guys!" Poppy interjected, her round cheeks flushed with pink over her wrinkles. "You can always tell. He's just got that look, you know? Like a white knight. And he's naming the initiative for Birdy in honor of all of Birdy's lobbying with state officials to guarantee that the spaceport will implement bird-friendly directives. It's just so exciting!" She clapped her hands together in delight. "And now I won't feel guilty when I take my seat on the first space flight!"

"You got your seat?" Luce asked.

"Yes!!" the older woman exclaimed. "Paddy gave me the ticket last night—it was his early Valentine's surprise for me!"

I gave Luce's hand a squeeze and planted a kiss on her cheek.

"A lot of that going around, it seems like," I whispered as a tingling sensation ran down my spine. *I was going to be a father. I was going to take my child birding. Wow.*

I pulled Luce away from the women and headed into the garage. I wanted a moment alone to hug my pregnant wife again.

And just as I wrapped my arms around her, a scream echoed in the garage and a giant kiskadee bolted by me, one hand slapping something hard into my stomach, its other hand dragging a screaming Pearl behind him.

The kiskadee threw Pearl into the green Porsche in the far stall of the garage, vaulted the hood of the sportscar, jumped into the driver's seat and reversed out at high speed. A screeching brake sound, a loud squeal of the tires, and the car went roaring away down Buzz's long driveway.

"Pearl!" Rosalie Pacheco screamed from the front of the garage. "He has Pearl!"

Ignoring the yells and chaos that had erupted in the garage, I looked at the hard object the kiskadee had stuck into my stomach and which now lay in my hands.

"What is that?" Luce asked, looking at the small weighted black sack I was holding.

"I'm not sure," I said.

"It's a sap," Chief Pacheco said, snapping a pair of handcuffs on my wrist. "And you're under arrest, Bob White, for assault with a deadly weapon and maybe a murder, too."

Chapter Twenty-Three

The next thing I knew, I was in the back of Pacheco's squad car looking out at Luce, who was surrounded by a clutch of MOBsters trying to comfort her.

Pacheco put on his lights and siren and roared out of the drive.

"I didn't do anything!" I yelled to the chief over the ear-splitting sound of the siren. "Luce was right there with me since we arrived. Ask anyone!"

"I know that!" Pacheco yelled back. "We're going after Buzz and Pearl!"

He pushed a keyring back to me through the screen behind him. "It's the key to the cuffs. Open 'em."

I reached forward and grabbed the keys. It took a minute or two for me to fit it in the lock—it's not like I usually get a chance to practice that little trick when I'm on birding trips, you know—and free my hands.

"So why am I here?" I shouted over the wailing that was still coming from the squad car. The chief took a corner, fast, and I had to grip the car door handle to keep myself from splaying out on my side.

I wondered if this was what it was like to drive with me when I was speeding.

"Because you were right there!" Pacheco called back.

He cut the siren, but not his speed. "You had the sap in your hand, and I needed an extra pair of eyes to keep up with Pearl and the bird. Look for the green Porsche!"

"There!" I shouted, "It hung a right two blocks ahead of us!"

The chief obliged.

"Gunnar," he told me, his voice rushed while he tore after the Porsche, "you know, the birder with the bandana around his head. Someone found him crumpled on the ground, unconscious, just as Pearl screamed. I checked his pulse, could see blood on his head, and I started running in her direction, but the bird had her. Then, I see you've got the sap in your hand, so I grab you to come with me."

"What's a sap?" I asked.

He spun the wheel again, and I grabbed at the back of the front seats to keep myself erect.

It didn't work. I ended up banging my shoulder against the car door.

"Put on the seat belt!" Pacheco commanded.

"Now you tell me," I complained, then complied, hurriedly locating the shoulder harness for the back right seat.

"The sap is what hit Gunnar," Pacheco shouted back to me. "It's what killed Birdy—it cracked his skull. You had the murder weapon in your hand. I wasn't about to lose it, so I took you along with it."

He pulled the squad car level with the Porsche. Luckily, most of the streets we'd flown through had been empty; the few cars on the road I had noticed in our mad dash had all pulled over when we came roaring by, courtesy of the blazing lights on top of the car. I looked out the window to see the back of the kiskadee's head and noticed a black eye patch dangling against the nape of his yellow neck.

Good to know that the kiskadee—Birdy's killer! Buzz?—was conscientious enough to remove the eye patch before racing around town at breakneck speeds with a kidnapped girl in his front seat with him.

Kidnapped.

Crap.

He'd kidnapped the Citrus Festival queen, who also happened to be the niece of the chief.

A really protective chief.

I got a really bad feeling about what was going to happen next.

A car shoot-out?

A hostage situation?

The Porsche suddenly pulled over and braked to a stop. Pacheco slid his squad car in front at an angle, blocking any forward progress the getaway car might make.

"Stay down!" the chief shouted at me as he jumped out and ran in a crouch around the front of the squad car, his service revolver in his hand.

I flattened myself on the back seat.

I heard car doors opening and slamming and Pearl shouting "Uncle Juan! Uncle Juan! Don't shoot!"

I braced myself for the inevitable sound of gunshots, but none came.

I counted to fifteen, then slowly lifted my upper body to peek out the back window.

Chief Pacheco stood on the sidewalk beside the Porsche with his left arm wrapped around his niece's shoulders, his gun trained across the top of the car on the giant kiskadee that stood next to the driver's open door. I peeled myself off the back seat and stepped out of the car to join Pacheco on the street. The chief pushed Pearl behind him and told me to get her into the squad car.

"Take off your head," I heard him order the kiskadee.

I glanced back in panic—had the chief said he was going to take off the kiskadee's head?

No, no, I heard it wrong, I realized as I watched the kiskadee reach his hands up to remove the head section of his costume.

Thank God.

No mob-style execution on the streets today, after all. This was Texas in the twenty-first century, not a black-and-white gangster movie set in 1930s Chicago.

And Pacheco had Birdy's killer: Buzz Davis, multi-millionaire, ex-astronaut, and Birdy's best friend.

The bird's head came off, but it wasn't Buzz Davis inside that kiskadee costume.

It was Mark Myers.

Chapter Twenty-Four

But you couldn't have killed Birdy," I blurted out, my hand resting on the doorframe after I'd stashed Pearl in the chief's car. "I saw you on Crazy Eddie's tape. You came to Estero Llano and then left right after Buzz and Birdy had gone into the park."

"I didn't kill Birdy," Mark said, his eyes locked on Pacheco's gun barrel. "He was my friend. He was about the only person around here who had any faith in me. But if it weren't for me," Mark seemed to choke up with emotion, "he might still be alive."

"He didn't kill Birdy," Pearl's voice sobbed from inside the car. "But we know who did. That's why we ran."

"I'm going to cuff you, Mark," Pacheco said, his voice hard. "If nothing else, you broke the law with your driving, and until I hear this whole story, I want you restrained."

Mark held up his feathered hands. "Cuff me. Please. There's nowhere I'd rather be right now than in the back seat of a squad car. Maybe then, Pearl and I can be sure we're going to make it through the day alive."

The chief holstered his gun and rounded the car to put handcuffs on Mark.

"Are you all right, Pearl?" I asked the queen, her tiara slightly askew, as she took several deep breaths and sniffed loudly to regain her composure after her sobbing had subsided. "What happened in the garage, anyway?"

Pearl adjusted her tiara, and smoothed her satiny dress over her waist. "Mark and I," she began, "we were, ah . . . well . . ."

She folded her hands in her lap and wouldn't look at me. "We were kissing a little behind the empty crates in the garage, and then we heard Gunnar start to say 'hello' to someone, but then there was an awful thud, and we heard a man saying 'Keep your mouth shut, permanently, you bozo,' and then," she broke off to look up at me, her eyes filling with tears.

"Mark put his hand over my mouth so I wouldn't make any noise, and no one would know we were there, because we were afraid of the man who said 'bozo', but Mark accidentally knocked a crate with his kiskadee tail, and it made a noise, and then we heard the man say 'who's back there?' in a very rough voice, and Mark grabbed my hand and we practically exploded out from behind the crates, and Mark almost knocked the man over, but he didn't, and then—"

I put up my hands in a "slow down" gesture to stop her frantic narration. By then, Pacheco had stuffed Mark in all his feathered glory into the seat beside Pearl and told me to get into the front passenger seat.

"So when you bumped into the guy, he tried to hit you with the sap, but instead, you grabbed it out of his hands and kept running," Pacheco said, apparently reciting back what Mark had just conveyed to him.

"Yes," both Mark and Pearl answered.

I noticed that Mark covered Pearl's hand with his own feathered one. She threw him a grateful glance and a small smile.

Oh, no, I thought. The boyfriend isn't going to like this. I remembered my introduction to Guardsman Pacheco at Fat Daddy's and the way he'd defended his Pearlita. The guardsman might find himself with some stiff competition from a white knight—or a Great Kiskadee, as the case happened to be—for Pearl's affections. Mark had, after all, whisked the queen away to safety.

Considering how fast he had been driving that Porsche, however, I'd say there was definitely more whisking than safety going on in that fair damsel's rescue.

"So who was it?" Chief Pacheco demanded of the two young people, twisting in his seat to interrogate them. "Who clobbered Gunnar? Who did you grab the sap from?"

The two youngsters looked at each other blankly, then at the chief.

"We don't know," Mark said. "I think I've seen him during the float building, but I don't know if I could pick him out of a crowd. Schooner's the only other birder I've hung out with, the only one I really recognize. When this guy tried to hit me with the sap, I wasn't going to ask for his name and address."

"He was one of the MOB," Pearl insisted. "I'm sure he's the one who wears flowered shirts a lot."

I put my head in my hands and groaned.

"They all do," I said. I turned to look at Pacheco as he pulled his radio from the dash and called in a report. When he was finished, I asked, "Your people will get fingerprints from the . . . what did you call it, again?"

"Sap."

"Right, sap," I said, immediately realizing the problem with that answer. "And they'll be my fingerprints, won't they?"

The chief nodded, pulling away from the curb. "Mark's fingers are covered with the costume, and I'm sure our killer is careful, and apparently experienced enough, to know to wear gloves when he uses a sap." He looked at me for a moment and actually smiled a little. "Unlike you, Bob White."

"What is a sap?" Pearl asked from the backseat.

"It's a little weighted ball inside a cloth sack," her uncle explained. "It's a weapon, and in the hands of someone who knows how to use it, it can kill someone by crushing the exactly right part of their skull. Our medical examiner determined that was what killed Birdy, but I didn't want anyone to know in hopes our killer would slip up and give himself away by mentioning a sap."

"Wait a minute," I said. "In the old gangster movies, didn't those guys carry saps?"

Pacheco shrugged, threading the squad car through quiet residential neighborhoods.

"Don't know," he said. "I didn't watch gangster movies when I was a kid. My mother thought they were too violent for children. We watched cartoons."

"So did I," Mark offered from the back seat. "Watching cartoons is what got me interested in fast cars and car chases."

I saw Pacheco give Mark a dirty look in the rear-view mirror.

"It's important," I muttered, more to myself than to the chief. An idea was tugging at the back of my mind, but I couldn't quite get it into focus. "I know it's important. Gangsters—mobsters—carrying saps. Didn't they threaten to use them on somebody who owed them money and didn't pay up? What was that called?"

"Collections?" Mark guessed, then changed the subject. "Is Gunnar dead?"

The boy's voice softened. "I don't think I can handle being responsible for two deaths."

The chief turned onto a gravel drive that led up to a one-story cream-colored adobe house. "Why do you say that, Mark? You didn't kill Birdy, so how is it your fault?"

I heard a masculine sniffle from the back seat.

"Because if I hadn't been late that morning, the morning that Birdy was killed, he wouldn't have been alone," Mark answered. "I'd promised to help him finish a surprise for Rosalie, and I was late, and I was embarrassed, because I'd been drinking the night before, and I didn't want him to know, because he's been . . ." Mark paused and sniffed again. "I didn't want to disappoint him after all the times he's stood up for me when I've screwed up with Uncle Buzz."

Pacheco stopped the car and told the two young people to get out and go in the house until he came back for them.

"Where are we?" Mark asked.

"It's my house. My grandma's home," Pearl told him. I heard her dress rustle and then her face was pressed up near the screen behind our front seats, her fingers splayed out on the metal mesh.

"I can't stay here, Uncle Juan," she pleaded with the chief. "I'm the Citrus Festival queen—I have to be in the parade!"

"You're also a witness to an assault and can possibly identify a murderer," he firmly told her. "You're staying here until I come and get you. Mark," he said, turning to the costumed boy, "I'm depending on you to keep her here. Do you understand me?"

Mark nodded. "She won't go anywhere."

Pearl burst into tears. "But I'm the queen! What will everyone say?"

"I can tell everyone you're under arrest for abetting a criminal," her uncle suggested.

Pearl gasped in disbelief. "You wouldn't!" she cried.

Pacheco nodded. "I would, if it meant keeping you safe."

"You can't!" the queen persisted.

I studied the faces of the uncle and niece, both equally set and stubborn.

Great. Another inter-generational family fight. What was it about these Texans, anyway? First Buzz and Mark, and now Pacheco and Pearl.

Family counselors had a goldmine in Texas, I decided.

"Look, you two," I said. "The parade doesn't start for another three hours, right?" I asked, checking my watch. "Maybe we can have the killer in custody in time for you to ride in the parade, Pearl. He's got to be flustered now, knowing we have the murder weapon, and that we have witnesses."

"But I don't know who he was!" Pearl insisted. "He's a birder, and that's all I know."

"But he doesn't know that," I reminded her. "He might think you've already named him, and that your uncle is closing in on him this very minute."

Pacheco tilted his head in acknowledgement of my conclusion. "Could be, Bob. All the more reason that I want Pearl here, and no one knowing about it. You're riding back to Buzz's garage with me, and by the time we get there, we're going to have this figured out."

He turned to Mark and Pearl. "Stay here until you hear from me. And no fooling around," he added, giving Mark a dark look.

Out of the blue, I thought about Luce being pregnant. The knowledge had totally escaped my mind in the heat of the chase, but now as I watched the two young people walk into the little house, all I could think of was: if I have a daughter, she's never going to be left alone in a house with a boy.

Even if he is dressed as a state specialty bird.

Especially if he's dressed as a state specialty bird.

"Okay, Bob," Pacheco said as he pointed the car back down to the main road of Mission, "it's time for you to prove to me that your exceptional memory for details is good for something other than identifying birds. You got a threatening note the night after working on the float, and Gunnar got sapped for not keeping his mouth shut, according to Mark and Pearl. What did Bandana Man say to you when you were building the float that could possibly lead us to a murderer?"

Chapter Twenty-Five

Ten minutes later, we were back at Buzz's garage, where the ambulance was just leaving. Two more squad cars were parked in the driveway in front of the MOB float. Pacheco had radioed ahead and told the deputies to stick around until he returned, in hopes they would be arresting Birdy's killer.

Unfortunately, the identity of that killer was still unknown, no matter how hard I tried to recall what Gunnar had said to me three nights ago. Only three topics of conversation stood out in my memory: Pacheco's protectiveness towards Rosalie and Pearl, Rosalie's disgust with immigration laws that had split up her family, and Paddy Mac's overactive imagination when it came to guessing about how Birdy might have died.

If I took Pacheco and Rosalie out of that list, that only left Paddy Mac and his streak of blarney. But if he'd killed Birdy, why would he say even a word to anyone about how it might have happened, let alone suggest a string of possible scenarios?

That didn't make any sense. Killers didn't want to be caught, and so far, Birdy's killer was doing a great job of it.

Except for almost giving himself away to Mark and Pearl in the garage.

I bet that shook him up plenty when he realized someone was within earshot of his attack on Gunnar. I wondered who was more spooked at that moment: the kids or the killer? That made me wonder something else: if the kids hadn't made any noise, would the killer have lingered another moment to hide Gunnar's body, as he'd tried to hide Birdy's body under the canoe?

Was this guy a clean-up freak?

Maybe that was why Luce and me had received the "go home" note—he might have considered us loose ends that might unravel his murder plot. Sending us scampering home would have gotten us neatly out of the way of his plans. At this point, I was fairly certain the killer had dismissed us as threats, since three days had passed since we'd been warned, and no identification of a killer had been forthcoming from us or anyone else. Clearly, Luce and I were as clueless to whatever mystery-solving information Gunnar may have unknowingly passed along as the chief was to why Birdy had been killed in the first place and Eddie had been shot at.

He—at least we knew that part now, that it was a he—must have been convinced Gunnar, or what Gunnar knew, warranted taking the chance to kill him in Buzz's garage. That must have taken nerve—there were plenty of people milling around, any of whom might have caught him in the act of attacking Gunnar . . . except that the sap was a silent weapon, and the damage it inflicted could be mistaken for an accidental impact blow. Paddy, who'd spent years working in insurance, had told us that accidents weren't uncommon around float construction areas.

Good job, Paddy, I thought ruefully, *you gave our at-large killer a perfect scenario for knocking off Gunnar.* Our killer had obviously taken that to heart, planning his attack on Gunnar for the final, somewhat chaotic, phase of float preparation.

Killing Gunnar was, then, a kind of insurance: without Gunnar, the last lead to the identity of Birdy's killer was gone, and he'd get away with murder.

Now that I thought about it some more, Paddy Mac had been creating scenarios for all kinds of mayhem in the last few days, according to Gunnar.

Was Paddy Mac a killer?

Or was the killer someone close to him who was secretly picking his brains to lay successful murder plans?

Yikes. I've heard of toxic friendships, but that one might just be over the top.

"Hey, Paddy, I'm thinking of committing murder. You got any good ideas for me to make it work?"

But if my theory about the drones being the real reason behind Birdy's death and Eddie's attack was correct, I was really going to have to come up with some fast creative thinking to connect Paddy Mac, or any of the birders, to it.

Fast creative thinking #1. Someone in the MOB was psychotically paranoid and thought the drone was spying on him, resulting in his uncontrollable compulsion to destroy the drone and the men working on it.

Huh. That wasn't too bad a theory for thinking on the fly. Maybe I could work with it.

I decided to try another.

Fast creative thinking #2. Someone in the MOB was dealing drugs and knew the drone was being primed to catch drug runners, resulting in the need to protect the business by killing off the drone and its operators.

But wouldn't another drone project just pop up in its place? Wrecking a program didn't sound like a permanent solution, but it could work as a temporary fix for the dealer, I supposed.

Okay, #2 wasn't totally bad, either, as long as the MOB dealer wasn't planning on being in the business long enough for the next drone project to get started. Given the advanced age of some of the MOBsters, maybe that wouldn't be a concern anyway. *Carpe diem*, and all that, you know.

The "go for the gusto" thing again.

Fast creative thinking #3.

Nothing. Nada.

I was out of fast creative thinking.

"Didn't you tell me you did background checks on all the MOB members?" I asked the chief as he put the squad car in park and turned off the engine.

"I did," he said. "And I found no criminal records."

"How about mental health records?"

The chief turned to face me. "What are you thinking? That we've got a nutcase taking out birders for the heck of it?"

I told him my two new motive theories. "So if any MOBster has a history of psychiatric care, don't you think that's worth looking at again?"

"At this point, I'll look under rocks if I have to," Pacheco said. "My niece is a murder witness." He spoke quickly into his radio. "I should hear back in a few minutes. I've got our researcher on it right now."

We got out of the car.

"Where's Pearl?" Rosalie cried, running to Pacheco as soon as she saw us.

I looked around for Luce, but didn't see her. I dug my cellphone out of my pocket to see if she'd called or left a message, but there was nothing.

"Where is she?" Rosalie demanded. "My Pearl. Tell me she is all right!"

Pacheco put his hands on his mother's shoulders and looked her in the eye. "Mom. Pearl is fine. She's safe. She's at the police station. She's giving a statement."

I was impressed: Pacheco was an excellent liar. If I hadn't been there and seen with my own eyes that he'd left Pearl at Rosalie's home, I never would have guessed the man was lying through his teeth about his niece's whereabouts. Under the circumstances, I decided Pacheco's deception was probably the most effective way to protect Pearl. As long as no one knew where she was, there was no chance anyone—in particular, Birdy's killer—could find her.

Protect . . . protection . . .

Protection racket!

That was it—the phrase I'd been looking for when I was thinking about mobsters collecting money in the old movies. Mark had said "collection," but it was "protection," as in Chicago-land mob honchos sending thugs to shake down shop owners for money, or else they beat up the owners with their saps and wrecked the store.

That was the phrase I'd been trying to remember, but now it didn't seem quite the right fit for whatever it was that was trying to break into my consciousness. I was certain I was getting closer to some piece of information that would point to Birdy's killer, but I just couldn't bring it into the sharpest focus.

I walked into the garage to find Luce.

"Bob!" Pacheco called to me from his car. "I got a call back. We have a hit!"

I gave him a thumbs up sign, but before I rejoined him to find out who our hot suspect was, I found Paddy Mac and asked him if he'd seen Luce.

Paddy flashed his big Irish grin. "Schooner took her inside the house after you left with the chief. He offered to sit with her until she heard from you."

He looked pointedly at my hands. "No cuffs. Luce said you were innocent. She told us that the kiskadee did it." He smiled again. "So who is he, Bob? Who killed Birdy?"

I decided to follow Pacheco's example.

I lied.

"We have no clue, Paddy."

At almost the same moment, Chief Pacheco snagged my shoulder and turned me to face him.

"It's Schooner," he said. "He's our hit."

I ran for the door into the house.

Chapter Twenty-Six

Luce!" I shouted as I burst into a polished oak hallway inside the garage door. "Luce!"

Voices came from the end of the hall, sending me at a run in their direction. I skidded through a doorframe and into a kitchen.

Luce was standing in front of a stovetop that was about five feet long, stirring something in a pan. I could hear sizzling noises and the aroma of roasted chicken and chili peppers hit me like a cresting ocean wave.

She looked up and frowned. "Are you all right, Bobby? I figured it was just a matter of time until you were able to convince the chief he was wrong about you, and you'd be back. Rosalie got me started on this taco filling to help me pass the time. She said she made it for Birdy for last Valentine's Day. Isn't that sad?"

Valentine's Day.

Why did that suddenly seem so important to me? Somewhere in my head, a bell was ringing.

Luce laid down the wooden spoon she'd been using and came to give me a hug. "Are you all right?" she repeated. "You don't look so good."

I didn't feel so good. There was a bell ringing in my head, and I'd just found my wife—my newly pregnant wife—calmly cooking chicken when I thought she might have been grabbed by a psycho killer. I guess I got a little concerned.

Like maybe my pregnant wife was going to get killed.

I kept Luce firmly enfolded against me for another minute.

"I love you," I whispered in her ear, relief and the adrenaline drop making my knees wobble beneath me. I kept holding on to her until I was sure I stopped shaking.

Luce pulled away in my arms and searched my face. "What is going on?"

"Where's Schooner?" Chief Pacheco demanded. He stood inside the kitchen door, his hand on the butt of the gun in his belt holster.

Luce looked from me to the chief.

"I'm right here," our fellow Minnesotan said, walking into the kitchen from an attached four-season porch. "You want me for something?"

"Yes," Pacheco said. "I need to ask you a few questions. After you." He motioned for Schooner to walk ahead of him back to the garage. "Let's go sit in my car for privacy."

The two men exited the room, and Luce left me to check on her chicken.

"We think there's a chance Schooner might be involved in Birdy's murder," I told Luce after I heard the door into the garage shut down the hallway. "Pacheco just found out that our MOBster from Duluth had some psychiatric problems in the past. It might explain why Birdy and Eddie were targeted if Schooner had some kind of—paranoia—about the drones."

Luce stirred the cooking meat and shook her head. "Schooner isn't psychotic, Bobby. He had PTSD when he came home from his combat duty tour in Vietnam back in the 1970s. He's had to get counseling and treatment over the years. He's a vet, like Birdy and Buzz. He told me all about it while you were gone."

She paused in her cooking and looked up at me. "It made the time go fast, especially since I had no idea what was going on with you and the chief. And I have a whole new appreciation for what some of our soldiers experienced in that war, Bobby. Schooner had been in those underground tunnels where the Viet Cong were hiding. He had to learn to move soundlessly, he said, or else he was risking having his head blown off."

"So he could certainly have snuck up on Birdy," I gently pointed out to her. I knew my wife: once she befriended someone, she was loyal to a fault. I didn't want her to kick herself later when we found out that Schooner's mental health problems had turned him into a killer.

"And if he was a soldier in combat," I reminded her, "he had hand-to-hand combat skills. The chief is doing his job, Luce, and the sooner he can identify Birdy's killer, the easier we can all breathe."

She laid the spoon down again and put a hand on her hip. "Didn't you guys go after Pearl and Mark? Pearl's a witness to a crime, isn't she? She'll be able to tell the chief who killed Birdy and shot at Eddie and tried to kill Gunnar."

For a moment, I was confused. I'd assumed that none of the people who'd seen me leave with the chief knew what had really happened in the garage with Mark and Pearl.

"How did you know it was Mark in the kiskadee costume?" I asked her. "And who said Pearl was a witness to a crime?"

"I did," Poppy Mac said, her head popping out from around the doorway into the four-season porch. I could hear the excitement in her voice. "Pearl knows who the killer is. That makes her a witness."

Witness.

The ideas tumbling around in my head suddenly fell into place and clicked together.

Protection.

That was it!

That was the odd piece of information Gunnar had given me, but he'd assumed it was a joke: Paddy Mac once said that he was in the witness protection program.

And, as far as I knew, only two types of people qualified for those programs: innocent people who needed protection from criminal retribution for their witness, and guilty people who got immunity from the law because they helped put guiltier people in prison.

Poppy had told us they'd moved around a lot, and she'd never gotten to know the neighbors.

And that Paddy used to work in collections, and that they had plenty of money.

Enough money, in fact, for Paddy to buy a ticket for a seat on the first commercial space ride for his wife as an early Valentine's gift.

A seat that had just opened up.

A seat, I realized now, that had belonged to Birdy Johnson, according to that framed news article I'd read in Fat Daddy's dining porch. Birdy and Buzz were going to be on that flight with the first passengers.

But now Birdy was dead, and his seat was going to someone else.

Poppy Mac.

What a coincidence.

I looked at Poppy's animated face, my adrenaline kicking back in.

I had a really bad feeling Paddy Mac was not the innocent type of witness protection person, and that his former job in collections wasn't about museum curating, as we had stupidly assumed.

Crap.

I got it now.

Paddy Mac had been an enforcer for a real mob, collecting protection money.

"Poppy," I said, sliding in front of Luce, all my instincts focused on protecting my wife and our newly unborn child. "The ticket for the spaceship that Paddy gave you—you were the first person on the waiting list, weren't you?"

Poppy nodded. "Yes! How did you know that?"

"He didn't, darlin'. I'm thinking he just put it all together, didn't you, Minnesota?"

I turned around to see Paddy Mac standing in the doorway to the hall.

He held a small gun pointed at my heart.

Chapter Twenty-Seven

I've always been much better with close-up work than long distance," he said, "so don't you be thinking I'll miss my shot at this close range the way I missed your friend Eddie, because I won't."

"And what then?" I asked him, mentally willing Luce to run from the room screaming for help. "You kill me, and then you're going to have two murder charges against you. Chief Pacheco is on to you, Paddy. He's got your sap and he's going to trace it to you with DNA. He's going to know you killed Birdy."

Yes, I lied. Again.

So sue me.

I bet if you were staring down the barrel of a gun, you'd lie, too.

Get out of here, Luce, I kept trying to message her.

What a time for her to forget to read my mind.

"Chief Pacheco has nothing on me," Paddy said, patiently, as if he were explaining something to a child, "and he's not going to find anything either, because Poppy and I have been in the witness protection program a long time. More than thirty years now, isn't it Poppy?"

I kept my eyes on his gun, but I caught sight of Poppy out of the corner of my eye. She was leaning against the far side of the kitchen island that stood between Luce and me and the four-season porch. She was clearly unconcerned that her husband held a gun in his hand.

"A little more than thirty, yes," she replied, tucking a strand of too-red hair behind her ears. "We've had so many moves since you testified against the mob. It's hard for me to keep track of the years, anymore. Let me see, after Chicago, we—"

Paddy cut her off.

I was almost grateful to him. The woman could talk you into a coma.

Maybe that was the real reason Paddy Mac refused to replace the bad batteries in his hearing aid. He didn't have to listen to his wife talk, because he couldn't.

Sometimes technology really is the solution, I guess.

"Poppy, be quiet, darlin'," he told her gently, his eyes and gun still locked on me. "You know, I thought it was funny, telling Gunnar the truth, because I knew he'd think I was joking."

I nudged Luce behind me with my elbow.

"Just goes to show you, you can't trust a man when he's drinking beer with you. You never know when he might remember what you told him." Paddy shook his head. "You should have gone home when I told you to, Minnesota."

"You left the note on our door," Luce said from behind me, her tone more angry than accusing.

No, no, no, honey, I cautioned her in my head. *Don't upset the nice old man with the gun in his hand. That would not be a good idea at this particular moment.*

"Why bother threatening us, Paddy?" Luce probed. "Why didn't you just shoot us in our bed at the Birds Nest if you were so worried we might figure out that you killed Birdy?"

Oh, great, I thought. *My wife is giving advice to a hit man.* Not only was she not reading my thoughts for once, but she was questioning a killer about his decisions.

I tried harder to mentally telegraph her.

What are you thinking, Luce? Get out of here!

Obviously, my wife was thinking about a lot of things, because the next words that came out of her mouth were: "And why did you shoot at Eddie if you killed Birdy for a seat into space? What did Eddie have to do with that?"

Paddy looked at my wife with surprise on his face.

"I was trying to clean up the mess I made," he said.

Ha! I was right. Again. The killer was a neat freak.

Not that it made me feel any better, at the moment. Especially since the neat freak killer still had a gun pointed at me.

"I heard someone coming in the woods, and didn't have enough time to pull the canoe all the way over Birdy's foot," Paddy explained. "I'd picked up the bottle the night before when Eddie left it at the garage. I stuck it in my pack, thinking I'd return it to him when I saw him again, but then I decided I could put it to better use if I left it by poor Birdy. I thought if I left the bottle, Eddie would take the rap."

A tiny squeak came from down the hall behind Paddy. I checked for a reaction in his eyes, but there wasn't any.

He didn't hear it.

His hearing aid hadn't picked it up.

Thank God for bad batteries.

"But if that was the plan," I asked him, hoping to gain precious seconds for whoever was, I had to believe, coming to our rescue, "why try to kill Eddie? You'd be ruining your own frame-up."

Paddy cocked his head to one side. For a split-second, I couldn't breathe.

Had he somehow sensed that there was someone creeping up behind him? Was I going to get a bullet in the next second?

No. Not yet.

Paddy Mac was smiling at me.

"I decided I'd rather frame Schooner," he said. "The man was a sharpshooter in Vietnam, you know, and I figured when the chief ferreted out that little piece of information, he'd figure Schooner was after both Birdy and Eddie. I had a little birdie of my own—make that a Poppy of my own," he amended, giving his wife a wink, "drop the hint that Schooner was involved with drug dealing. It's just a hop, skip, and a jump then for the chief to conclude that Schooner had a motive to kill those other two—he was trying to end the drone project to protect his own illegal business."

"Oh, no," Poppy said, from the far side of the kitchen island. "I was supposed to say it was Schooner? I thought I was supposed to say that Mark was the one involved with drugs. You told me to say it was Mark, Paddy, so that's what I told Bob and Luce here at the gift shop. You mean I got it wrong?"

Paddy shot her a glance, but the gun in his hand remained trained on me.

"Why would you say it was Mark, when I distinctly told you to say Schooner?"

I heard another squeak in the hallway. Help was getting closer.

Paddy was still oblivious, and I needed him to stay that way for just a moment longer.

So for once in my life, I decided to not break up a fight.

I stopped being a counselor.

"Why did you say Mark, Poppy?" I asked her, my eyes still on Paddy's face. "Why didn't you do what he told you to do?"

"I did!" Poppy insisted from behind me. "He didn't tell me to say Schooner, he told me to accuse Mark!"

Paddy turned his head to yell at his wife. "I said to accuse the mark, woman! Schooner was *the* mark, not Mark!"

As soon as Paddy's attention left me for his wife, I whirled, shoving both Luce and myself around the edge of the kitchen island and taking us to the floor. I heard a gunshot and then another.

"Paddy!" Poppy cried out.

I could hear scuffling near the stovetop, Poppy crying, and the sound of jostling bodies.

"Minnesota, are you all right?"

I looked up from where I was covering Luce with my body on the floor to see Schooner standing over us.

"We've got Paddy," he said, extending a hand to help me up. "You're safe. Both of you."

"You were the one coming down the hall," I guessed, standing up and pulling Luce upright and into my arms for a smothering hug.

"I love you," I whispered into her ear. I turned to Schooner. "Luce said you knew how to move soundlessly and, man, that was exactly what we needed. Thanks."

"No problem," Schooner nodded in acknowledgement. "Some things you never forget," he said. "It's nice when one of those things turns out to be helpful, and not just one more recurring bad dream."

He smiled then, moving the conversation on and away from what I suspected involved his PTSD history and his memories of war.

"Although," he said, "those couple of squeaks in the hallway sounded like sonic booms to me. Anyone other than Paddy would have heard those squeaks. All I could do was pray he hadn't replaced those bad batteries yet."

On the other side of the room, Chief Pacheco and two deputies were cuffing Paddy and Poppy Mac. I thought I heard Poppy apologizing fervently to Paddy for getting her instructions mixed up, but Paddy was ignoring her.

Or he couldn't hear her. Or maybe both.

"Hey, Minnesota," Schooner said, clapping his hand on my shoulder, "how about I get you and your lovely wife a nice cold glass of the best fresh-squeezed orange juice you've ever tasted, and then we go cheer on the best MOB float you've ever seen?"

I looked in the eyes of the man who'd saved our lives and smiled. "Well, I have to tell you, it's the first MOB float we've ever seen, but I have no doubt, it's going to be the best."

I put my hand out to shake his. "Thanks, Schooner. You're a good man. One of the best, yourself."

He shook my hand. "My pleasure, Minnesota."

"So where's Pearl?" Luce asked. "Did you and the chief take her and Mark to the parade starting point before you came back here?"

Crap!

I'd totally forgotten that the kids were marooned out at Rosalie's house for safe-keeping. How could there be a Citrus Festival Parade without its Queen?

"Let's go," I said to Luce, grabbing her hand and starting for the door to the hallway. "Chief, I'm going to go get Pearl!" I shouted across the room to Pacheco. He looked up briefly and nodded.

"We need statements," he called back. "We can do it here later."

We headed out to the garage, where Buzz and Rosalie were in the center of a group of birders, all of whom seemed unusually quiet. They reminded me of a handful of birds in a bush that suddenly go silent when a hawk flies by.

Hearing gunshots inside a house will probably do that to you, I figured.

As soon as they caught sight of Luce and me, however, the group broke out into a barrage of questions.

"What happened?"

"Did anyone get hurt?"

"Where's the chief?"

"Who all was in there?"

"The chief will let you know," I told them. "We've got to retrieve Pearl and get her to the parade start."

Buzz stepped out of the crowd and handed me a keyring.

"Take the Mustang," he said. "Pearl wanted to use it for the parade, anyway. After what she's been through this morning, she deserves to ride in style."

He cast a glance back in Rosalie's direction and smiled. "I have a feeling Mark would be happy to be her designated driver."

Then, his eyes shimmered with unshed tears.

"Thanks, Bob. For everything," he added.

"Any time, Buzz."

I turned to my wife and held out the keyring. "I think you should drive, Luce."

Her eyes lit up and she snatched the keyring from my fingers.

"You got that right, Minnesota," she grinned. "Let's fly."

Chapter Twenty-Eight

I got Rosalie's address from Buzz and put it into my phone GPS. Luce slid into the driver's seat and turned the key in the ignition. When that big V-8 roared to life the look on her face was about as blissful as I've ever seen it.

The woman sure loved her cars.

Did they make infant car seats for classic Mustangs?

I couldn't wait to find out.

In the meantime, though, we had a queen and her white knight to pick up.

"Take a left, Luce," I told her, and we glided smoothly out of the neighborhood.

With the Mustang's top down, the sun was warm on our faces and a light breeze carried the scent of lemons and oranges into the car.

"So, did you get what you wanted out of this trip?" I asked my wife as we drove out to Rosalie's house to pick up the kids. "Sunshine, heat, lemons and birds?"

"I did," she assured me. "I got it all. Mission accomplished . . . and then some."

She threw me a happy glance. "How about you, Bobby? Did you get what you wanted?"

I gazed at my wife behind the wheel of Mark's Mustang. She was as beautiful as ever.

And she was carrying our first child.

"Yup," I said. "Aside from a murder, a shooting, an almost-arrest, a car chase, and being held at gunpoint, it was pretty darn satisfying as far as a birding vacation goes."

I leaned over and gave her a kiss on the cheek.

"Mission accomplished," I said, patting her on the belly, "and then some."

Bob White's Bird List for *Kiskadee of Death*

Ruddy Duck
Sora
Gadwall
Common Gallinule
American Coot
Mottled Duck
Blue-winged Teal
Green-winged Teal
Vermilion Flycatcher
Yellow-crowned Night-Heron
Green Kingfisher
Great Kiskadee
Plain Chachalaca
Golden-fronted Woodpecker
Black-crested Titmouse
Buff-bellied Hummingbird
Northern Mockingbird
Inca Dove
White-tipped Dove
Turkey Vulture
Eastern Screech-Owl
Couch's Kingbird
Great-tailed Grackle
White-eyed Vireo
Yellow-bellied Sapsucker
White-winged Dove
Orange-crowned Warbler
Rufous Hummingbird
Curve-billed Thrasher
Red-crowned Parrot
Gray Hawk
Green Jay
Altamira Oriole
Eared Grebe
White Ibis

Acknowledgements

Researching and writing this book has literally opened new horizons for me, since I'd never visited the Lower Rio Grande Valley before I met Nancy Millar at a Birding Diversity Conference several years ago. Nancy, a dynamo who is the vice-president of the Convention and Visitors Bureau of the McAllen, Texas, Chamber of Commerce, invited me to come to McAllen and see for myself why it's such a world-class birding site, and so I did. (Of course, it didn't hurt that there was almost a one hundred degree difference in temperatures between Minnesota and Texas when I left for McAllen in January 2014.) My visit convinced me I had to set my next Birder Murder Mystery there, and I am indebted to Nancy for introducing me to the area, the culture, and the many new friends I met there.

Rhonda Gomez is one of those friends, as well as my go-to source for good restaurant recommendations and my hostess at the Birds Nest in McAllen. Keith Hackland, the owner of the Alamo Inn, was my charming and informative host in Alamo, where I met fellow Minnesota birder Gunnar Berg, whose name, along with his Hawaiian shirt, I have borrowed for one of my characters. Carlos Rivas, superintendent at Texas Parks and Wildlife Department, graciously answered my questions about legal jurisdiction along the Lower Rio Grande Valley and clarified some immigration points for me. Sarah Williams, the executive director of Frontera Audubon, tipped me off to the SpaceX project, which became such a key piece of *Kiskadee of Death.* Finally, I have to add the folks at Shipley Do-Nuts to my thank-you list for my personal tour of the McAllen store, and yes, the Bavarian cream-filled doughnuts are awesome.

Here in Minnesota, I have another crew to thank for their contributions to my crafting my manuscript. Thanks to Joe Byrnes for sharing with me his true story about almost getting arrested at Falcon Dam in Texas. Sharon Stiteler, the Birdchick, sent me to Fat Daddy's in Weslaco when I told her I was going to visit the nine

World Birding Centers along the Lower Rio Grande Valley. My team at North Star Press—Corinne, Curtis, and Anne—continue to keep me on task and inspire me to make each book better—I am honored to work with them and be a part of the North Star family.

As always, I am incredibly grateful to my family for all the support they give me in my writing career. A big round of applause goes to my son Bob for checking my manuscript for avian accuracy, in addition to being so patient with his mother as I continue to develop my own birding skills and store of knowledge. As for my husband Tom, there will never be enough words to thank him properly for everything he contributes to my ability to pursue this writing passion of mine. I am truly blessed in every way.

Finally, I want to acknowledge all my readers for joining me on this Birder Murder Mystery ride. Your comments and suggestions are always appreciated, and you make my day when you let me know how much you've enjoyed Bob White and his adventures. I hope you'll continue to share your enthusiasm with others, encouraging all of us to look at our great outdoors with new eyes.

Good birding to all!